"What's wrong?" His gaze swept her up and down as if searching for injuries. "Did you get cut on a tree branch or something?"

He put his hands on her shoulders, his fingers gently sliding down each sleeve of her jacket, testing for rips. If she was the crying type, she'd have been a puddle on the ground by now. When he didn't find any holes in the fabric, he put his hands on her shoulders again.

"Piper? What is it?"

"There aren't any more tire tracks to follow. We're utterly lost. I'm so, so sorry, Colby. I think I've killed us both." A sob burst from her and she covered her face with her hands. So much for not being a crier.

His arms crushed her against him as he rested his cheek on top of her head.

"Shh, it's okay," he whispered. "None of this is your fault. It's okay."

She shamelessly allowed him to comfort her for one long, selfish minute, reveling in the feel of his strong arms around her.

STRANDED WITH THE DETECTIVE

Lena Diaz

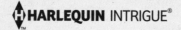

In 2017, Harlequin Intrigue lost a gifted author. The world lost a generous, caring soul. This book is dedicated to the memory of Paula Graves. Thank you, Paula, for the cat advice and for the privilege of letting me include a reference to your Chief Massey of Bitterwood P.D. in my very first Destiny, Tennessee, SWAT book, *Tennessee Takedown*. It was such fun sharing our fictional worlds. You will be missed.

ISBN-13: 978-1-335-52642-7

Stranded with the Detective

Copyright © 2018 by Lena Diaz

PLEASE RECYCLE

THIS PRODUCT IS RECYCLABLE

Recycling programs for this product may not exist in your area.

Printed in U.S.A.

HARLEQUIN®

™ www.Harlequin.com

Lena Diaz was born in Kentucky and has also lived in California, Louisiana and Florida, where she now resides with her husband and two children. Before becoming a romantic suspense author, she was a computer programmer. A Romance Writers of America Golden Heart® Award finalist, she has also won the prestigious Daphne du Maurier Award for Excellence in mystery and suspense. To get the latest news about Lena, please visit her website, lenadiaz.com.

Books by Lena Diaz

Harlequin Intrigue

Tennessee SWAT

Mountain Witness
Secret Stalker
Stranded with the Detective

Marshland Justice

Missing in the Glades
Arresting Developments
Deep Cover Detective
Hostage Negotiation

The Marshal's Witness
Explosive Attraction
Undercover Twin
Tennessee Takedown
The Bodyguard

Visit the Author Profile page at Harlequin.com.

CAST OF CHARACTERS

Piper Caraway—This horse ranch owner from Kentucky is struggling to keep her ranch afloat because of all kinds of mishaps that are sinking her finances. But are these coincidences or is someone behind all the problems?

Colby Vale—Destiny, Tennessee, SWAT officer and detective. A trip to the county fair puts him in the middle of a horse thief case and right into the problems that Piper Caraway is experiencing. But if she's as innocent as she seems, why is she suddenly a target for murder?

Wayne Wilkerson—His former horse ranch borders Piper's. Did he really want to sell his business, or does he blame Piper for all his troubles and want revenge?

Todd Palmer—He's caused Piper nothing but trouble. But is her prize stallion all he wants, or does he have far more sinister plans for her and Colby?

Jedidiah—When Piper and Colby find themselves in a tight spot in the middle of the Appalachian Mountains, this man and his thugs cause nothing but problems for the duo. Was it a "wrong place, wrong time" kind of thing? Or does Jedidiah have something to do with the problems on Piper's ranch?

Aunt Helen—She was Piper's surrogate parent after the death of her biological parents. But when Piper became an adult and took back the ranch, did she create an enemy of the woman who ran the ranch for so many years?

Billy Abbott—He managed the ranch for Aunt Helen. Now that Piper has control, does he resent her interference? Or is he worried that she might discover what he's really been doing with the ranch's funds?

Sheriff Jamie O'Leary—He's supposed to be the law and help Piper. But so far he's done next to nothing to discover who might be behind all the troubles on the ranch. Is he incompetent? Or does he have a secret connection to Piper's dead parents?

Ken Taylor—A new hire, he's supposed to provide security for the ranch. But ever since he came on board, there's been nothing but trouble. Could he be the cause?

Chapter One

Piper leaned around the edge of the tent that enclosed the temporary stables and curled her fingers around her pocketknife. Ahead and to the left, two more enormous tents partially concealed the winter-brown field that formed the fair's makeshift parking lot. And, of course, the truck and horse trailer that she specifically wanted to see were in the part of the lot that she *couldn't* see. Was Palmer still trying to figure out what she'd done to his truck? Or had he fixed it as soon as he'd popped the hood? Maybe she should sneak back to see whether her diversion was working.

No. Too risky. If he saw her, that would ruin everything. She needed to trust her plan, give it one more minute to make sure he didn't come right back. Then she could duck inside and take what was rightfully hers.

The area in front of the stables was mostly empty except for a few stragglers by the food trucks. Most of the people were in the bleachers a hundred yards away, erected for the weeklong event on the outskirts of a little town called Destiny, Tennessee.

Its entire population could have fitted several times

over inside Rolex Stadium at the Kentucky Horse Park back home. Tucked into the foothills of the Smoky Mountains, Destiny was smack-dab in the middle of Blount County. She supposed the central location made it the perfect spot for the fair because it would draw people from all over the state.

The distant rumble of engines signaled the beginning of the smash-'em-up derby, the main event. The audience was probably freezing as they huddled together, watching fools crunch cars into each other while speeding around a dirt track. Bumper cars for adults. Not Piper's idea of fun, especially early in the morning, in forty-degree weather.

A metallic bang had the crowd cheering. She shook her head in bemusement. Tucking her chin into the collar of her hooded jacket, she watched two couples approach a food truck. One of them was pushing a pink baby stroller piled high with blankets. A lone man trailed a few steps behind, obviously with them but the expression on his face clearly said he'd rather *not* be.

Piper smiled in commiseration. This was the last place she wanted to be, too.

Maybe a hairbreadth shy of six feet, the loner had thick coal-black hair that reminded her of the mane on one of her bays. It was a shame he kept it so short, not that it wasn't attractive cut that way. The style accentuated the sharp angles of his face, his strong jaw.

He wore a hip-length jacket, but it did little to conceal his thick biceps or the way his muscular thighs filled out his worn blue jeans. He looked fit and strong, the kind of man who could easily control even the most stubborn of stallions. But there was an innate gentleness in his easy smile as he bent over the baby stroller that spoke of a kind heart. Piper couldn't imagine him wielding a whip to force a recalcitrant horse to bend to his will.

She shook her head at her silly thoughts. His dark good looks definitely appealed. But making assumptions about his temperament based on appearance was just as foolish as judging a Thoroughbred without running it around a track. It was also a waste of time. Why had she become so fixated on him when she should have sneaked into the tent by now?

The answer hit her like a fist to the stomach.

It was that black jacket that he was wearing, and the fact that his two male friends, and even the blonde woman without the baby stroller, wore the same kind of jackets.

Exactly the same.

The hair prickled on her arms. All four exuded an air of confidence and authority, of temporarily banked power, ready to spring into action at the slightest provocation. Behind the smiles and laughs, there was a guardedness about their posture, as if they were keeping a well-practiced eye out for trouble, hyperaware of their surroundings.

Just like police officers did.

That would explain the matching jackets. She'd bet the overdue mortgage payment on her ranch that those jackets were reversible, and if you turned them inside out, they'd have words printed on the back, something like *Destiny Police Department*.

Her hand tightened around her knife.

There's nothing to see here. Keep moving. Go watch the silly car bashing on the other side of the field.

The couple with the stroller stopped at a cotton candy booth about thirty feet from Piper's hiding place. The other couple didn't seem lovey-dovey like the first. It dawned on her that maybe, since they were wearing matching jackets that screamed "cop," they were just coworkers out having fun rather than a couple. But the loner of the group—the dark-haired man she'd been admiring earlier—stood a short distance away from the rest of them, arms crossed over his chest.

In spite of the brisk air, a bead of sweat trickled between Piper's breasts. Had she thought him kind looking before? Because now the concentration and focus on his face as he studied his surroundings seemed almost lethal, dangerous, like a feral predator looking for his next meal.

His head suddenly swiveled toward her. She sucked in a breath and jerked back around the corner.

Stupid, stupid. She shouldn't have stood there so long. It wasn't like she was seventeen again, crushing on the high school quarterback. High school was six years ago, a lifetime ago. And she had far more important things to worry about—like salvaging her livelihood, and the livelihoods of everyone who worked for her. She couldn't let them down. Had he seen her? Did she look as guilty as she felt? Cops had a sixth sense about things.

She listened intently for the sound of his boots against the hard-packed dirt coming toward the tent. Her heart hammered so hard she could hear it pulsing in her ears.

Calm down. No one knows what you're about to do. Not even hot-cop.

A sharp whinny sounded from inside the tent. Piper's breath caught. She knew that beloved whinny. Tears sprang to her eyes. She drew a shaky breath, then another. There were no sounds of footsteps approaching. Maybe he hadn't seen her after all, or hadn't been concerned if he had. If she was going to do this, she had to do it now. She was all out of options and this was her run for the roses.

The whinny sounded again.

She flipped open the knife, then slipped into the tent.

COLBY TRUDGED ALONG behind the SWAT team leader and fellow detective, Dillon Gray, and Dillon's wife, who was pushing their sleeping six-month-old daughter in a stroller. The other two fellow detectives and SWAT officers with them, Blake and Donna, had hurried ahead to save seats at the derby. But hurrying was the last thing that Colby wanted to do. He was content to let the space between him and the Grays get longer and longer. Being the third wheel, or fifth wheel in this case, wasn't exactly at the top of his "how I wanted to spend my Saturday" list.

Plan A had been to play couch potato and watch a rerun of last year's Super Bowl. But his well-meaning friends, who were worried that he was "moping" over his recent breakup with his girlfriend, had forced him to dump Plan A. Plan B was to sneak out of the fair and go back home. Unfortunately, from the way Dillon kept looking over his shoulder, Plan B wasn't looking too promising.

So much for a relaxing weekend.

His friends meant well, which was the only reason he'd given in to their pestering to come here. But their concern was hardly necessary. Colby and his ex-girlfriend had parted on good terms, mutually agreeing that they were better suited as friends than lovers. Neither of them was suffering over the breakup and she was already dating someone else. Just because Colby hadn't started a new relationship yet didn't mean that he was unhappy. But Dillon's matchmaking wife, Ashley, couldn't accept that he could be happy alone. And her ridiculously love-smitten husband ruthlessly used his position as lead detective and head of the SWAT team to force Colby to go along with Ashley's wishes.

Judging by the occasional commiserating looks that Blake had shot him this morning, Colby was certain that he didn't want to be here either. But Blake was still new to the team and was having a hard time fitting in. So he wasn't about to put up a fuss. The SWAT team was going to the fair and then to a cookout at Max's house, yet another member of their team, whether they wanted to or not. Dillon had decreed it.

Colby hunched into his police-issued jacket, grateful for the insulated lining that kept him relatively warm. The smell of buttery popcorn carried across the cold breeze that blew through the pine trees. Maybe he could snag a bag later to eat while he watched the recording of that football game. If he was ever allowed to go home.

Slowing his steps even more, he glanced longingly

at his brand-new dark blue 4x4 Chevy pickup parked in a field of weeds that had been transformed into a parking lot for the week. But when he looked back toward his friends, he saw that they'd stopped. Dillon was facing him, right hand on his hip, about where his holster rested beneath his jacket. Colby rolled his eyes at the empty threat but plodded forward anyway.

The wind blew again, bringing with it something new—a sound. Something that didn't fit with the crowd noise in the distance or the vendors restocking for the rush they expected after the derby.

He stopped and turned around. What had he heard? The scuffling of feet against dirt? Muted voices? A muffled argument? Something had the little hairs standing up on his arms and the back of his neck, and it wasn't the wintry air. Had the sound come from the huge burlap tent about fifty feet away?

He'd noticed someone standing there earlier, their features concealed beneath a dark blue hooded jacket. But they'd ducked back when he'd looked their way. He'd been tempted to confront them, to see whether they were up to no good. But Ashley had distracted him by asking him a question. By the time he'd looked back toward the stranger, they'd disappeared.

The person he'd seen was probably just one of the handlers or one of the riders. When the derby and intermission were over, there was going to be a parade of horses to entertain the crowds. Ribbons and prize money would be handed out for a variety of categories. And after that there would be a horse race, one of the main reasons that Dillon had wanted to come.

Horses were his life outside the SWAT team and his detective work.

Colby had grown up in Destiny just like Dillon. And since it seemed like every other house outside town had horses, including Colby's family, he knew his way around them just as well as anybody. But that didn't mean he wanted to hang around them in his off time. He'd much rather nurse a beer and put his feet up while he cheered on his favorite football team, even if it was a rerun.

Man, he'd really wanted to watch that game today.

When he didn't hear anything else, he turned around and jogged toward Dillon.

A high-pitched scream sounded behind him.

Colby whipped around. Another scream rang out. It had come from the tent where he'd seen the hooded figure. He yanked his gun out of the holster and took off in a dead run.

Chapter Two

Colby stopped just inside the makeshift stables, holding his pistol down by his side. There were two aisles of wooden stalls, enough to hold about twenty horses. He could see the horses' graceful heads arching above the sides of the stalls, many of them snorting or stamping their hooves in agitation. A string of lights ran overhead down the center of each aisle. He edged forward, listening intently, every muscle tense and ready for action.

A whimper sounded down the left aisle.

"Oh, for goodness' sake," a voice hissed. "Grow a pair."

Two people were visible through the wooden slats of the next-to-last stall. One of them was maybe a couple inches over five feet, wearing the blue hooded jacket he'd seen earlier. The other man towered nearly a foot over him, his broad shoulders encased in a dark jacket, a green baseball cap perched on top of his head.

Colby crept down the aisle. He'd almost reached the open stall door when the larger man screamed. A knife glinted in the overhead light between them.

Colby sprang into the opening, swinging his gun toward the tall man holding the knife. "Police, freeze."

The knife wielder's eyes widened and he immediately dropped the knife in the straw at his feet.

"Officer, it's not what you—oomph." He fell to the ground, writhing in pain and cupping his hands between his legs. The smaller man, the one wearing the hood, had just slammed his shoe into the other man's groin.

Colby winced in sympathy and holstered his gun. He stepped into the stall and the smaller man kneeled over the one on the ground and drew his fist back.

Colby yanked him to his feet before he could take the swing.

"What part of *freeze* and *police* did you *not* understand?" He shook the man.

His hood fell back and a mass of glossy brown hair fell out, tumbling down his back. Correction. *Her* back. Dark green eyes glittered up at him under perfectly shaped brows that formed an angry slash.

Colby hesitated, his hands on her shoulders. Even with her face scrunched in fury, she was one of the most beautiful women he'd ever seen. Her long lashes framed catlike eyes and cheekbones a model would have killed for. An adorable smattering of freckles danced across her sun-bronzed cheeks. Pink, plump lips gave her a sexy, sultry appearance that had his mouth going dry.

"Let me go," she demanded, trying to wriggle free.

"Don't let her hurt me," the man on the floor gasped, still clutching himself.

Colby cleared his throat and let the woman go, taking a much-needed step away from her to look down at the man lying in a pile of hay. The knife lay beside him. Colby swiped it with his boot, sending it skittering out into the aisle.

"I'm Officer Colby Vale," he said. "I heard someone scream." He glanced from the large man to the petite woman.

"Well, it sure wasn't me," she snapped.

It took every ounce of control that Colby possessed not to smile at the gorgeous, infuriated hellcat. She looked incredibly insulted at the idea that she might have screamed.

The man in the hay coughed, his face turning bright red. "She had a knife," he said, as if to explain, his voice coming out in a plaintive whine.

"You were the one with a knife when I got here," Colby said.

"I'd just taken it away from her!" He pointed at the woman.

She rolled her eyes. "You got lucky. And it's not like I came at you with the knife or anything. I was using it to cut the cruel bindings you'd put on Gladiator. He could barely breathe."

"It was for his own safety," the man argued. "He kept slamming himself against the sides of the stall. I had to tie him to keep him from getting hurt."

"Wait, Gladiator?" Colby asked. "We're talking about a horse? Which one?"

Both of them pointed to the next stall, the last one in the aisle.

Colby turned and his mouth literally dropped open when he saw the stallion. Jet-black, it had a thick, glossy mane that rippled over its withers. Its proud, high tail was just as glossy and thick and probably

swept the floor. The animal appeared to be a cross between some kind of draft horse and a Thoroughbred.

"What's the breed?" he asked.

"Friesian." The woman's voice was full of pride.
"Gorgeous, isn't he?"

"Incredible." Colby looked at the man on the ground.
"Can you stand?"

He pushed himself to his feet, swaying. Colby
thought he might have to catch him. But then the man
grabbed the top rail and steadied himself.

"What's your name?" Colby asked.

"Todd Palmer." He pointed at the woman. "I want
you to arrest her."

"You were the one with the knife," Colby reminded
him.

Palmer started to say something, but Colby held
his hand up to stop him. "Hold it." He looked at the
woman. "What's your name?"

Her mouth tightened, as if she was considering not
answering. But then she grudgingly said, "Piper."

A flash of sunlight stabbed down the aisle as the
tent's front flap lifted. Blake and Dillon both rushed
inside. Colby waved them over.

"It's all right," he told them. "Everything's under
control." He eyed Piper, who reminded him of a rabid
badger ready to attack. This time he didn't even try to
hold back his smile. "More or less."

Her eyes narrowed dangerously.

God help him, Colby stirred the hornet's nest.
He winked.

Her eyes widened, then narrowed again and she
crossed her arms over her generous chest.

Dillon cleared his throat, giving Colby a curious look before picking up the knife from the ground. "Anybody hurt? We heard a scream. Several, actually." He looked at Piper. "You okay, ma'am?"

She snorted.

Dillon arched his brows. "What am I missing?"

"*She's* not the one who screamed." He gestured toward Palmer. "*He* is."

As one, Dillon and Blake turned toward Palmer. At least six feet two inches tall, he had the build of a lumberjack. His adversary was five feet, at the most. And she looked like a hard wind could blow her down. And yet, she'd been the one who was winning their little fight when Colby had confronted them.

"O…kay." Dillon glanced back and forth as if trying to figure out how in the world a tiny woman could terrorize the giant of a man.

Colby wanted to know the same thing.

Blake coughed behind his hand, obviously trying not to laugh.

"Let's start over." Colby took a step back while Dillon pocketed the knife. "We're detectives and SWAT officers for the Destiny Police Department."

"I hate always being right," the woman grumbled beneath her breath.

Colby didn't have a clue what she meant. Pointing to his right, he said, "This is my boss, SWAT team leader and Lead Detective Dillon Gray." He gestured to his other side. "This is Detective Blake Sullivan. I'm Detective Colby Vale. Dillon, Blake, the gentleman there says he's Todd Palmer. I haven't checked his ID yet."

"I'll take care of that." Blake held out his hand. "Sir, if you'll give me your driver's license, I'll run a few quick checks, make sure we're all friends here."

His smile was friendly, his words disarming, but there was a thread of steel beneath them that brooked no argument. Palmer handed over his license with obvious reluctance. Blake held it so that Dillon and Colby could read it before he pocketed it.

"I'm not some criminal with an outstanding warrant or something," Palmer complained.

"Excellent. That'll make my job much easier." Blake held his hand out toward Piper. "Ma'am? ID?"

She blew out an impatient breath but did as he asked, pulling her driver's license from the back pocket of her jeans.

Colby read the full name on the card as she handed it to Blake. "Piper Caraway. You and Mr. Palmer are both from Kentucky?"

Blake headed up the aisle with their IDs.

"I don't know where he's from," Piper answered, aiming a glare at Palmer. "But I'm from Lexington, or right outside it anyway, Meadow County. Look, all you need to know is that he stole my horse and I'm here to take it back. If anyone needs to be arrested here, it's him."

Palmer drew himself up as if trying to look more imposing. But the effect was ruined by the smattering of straw stuck to the side of his head. From the smell coming off him, Colby had a feeling there was a fair share of horse manure in that straw. He wrinkled his nose and took a quick step back. Dillon wasn't as subtle.

He waved his hand in front of his nose and gave Palmer a disgusted look.

"He stole your horse?" Colby asked Piper. "The one you called Gladiator?"

"He sure did. It took me weeks to figure out where he'd taken him. I chased them halfway across the South."

"I did *not* steal that horse." He reached inside his coat pocket.

Suddenly two pistols were pointing at him, Dillon's and Colby's.

Palmers eyes widened and beads of sweat popped out on his forehead. "I just wanted to show you the bill of sale."

"Hold still." Dillon holstered his gun and patted Palmer down while Colby aimed his pistol at the ground.

"He's clear," Dillon announced. He pulled a sheaf of papers out of the man's inside jacket pocket as Colby holstered his gun again. "Is this what you wanted to show us?"

"Yes." Palmer waved toward Piper. "It's my employer's bill of sale, Wayne Wilkerson. He owns the place next to the Caraway ranch and had me bring over the bill of sale to pick up Gladiator on his behalf. Aren't you going to search her, too?"

"Colby will take care of that." Dillon studied the papers.

"While you're at it," Palmer snarled, "you can charge her with vandalism or something. My truck alarm went off in the parking lot and I found it with the hood up. I didn't see any damage or anything missing, so I tried to start the engine to make sure everything was okay. It wouldn't start. Took me thirty minutes to figure out that someone had shoved a rubber washer onto the battery post to block the electric current. It doesn't take a brainiac to figure out who's responsible."

"Thank goodness, since that would completely disqualify you," Piper snapped.

Colby hid his smile by rubbing the light line of stubble that ran up the sides of his face to his hairline.

Palmer's face reddened and he took a threatening step toward Piper.

The woman had the audacity to take an answering step toward him.

Colby swore and jerked her back to a safe distance while Dillon stepped between them.

"Cool it, or I'll slap you in cuffs," Dillon ordered, addressing Palmer. "And it'll be that much longer before we straighten out this mess."

Palmer glared at Piper, his earlier fear of the knife apparently forgotten. But he didn't try to approach her again.

Dillon arched a brow at Colby, an unsubtle reminder to do his job.

Feeling his face flush with heat for letting his professionalism slip yet again around the intriguing woman, he told her, "Ma'am, I need to check you for weapons. Tempers are obviously running high around here and we don't want any firearms getting in the mix."

"I'm not armed," she said but suffered through the frisk without complaint.

Everything about her posture and expression screamed that *she* was the wronged party, making Colby feel like a jerk for touching her. If Palmer—or his alleged employer, Wilkerson—had stolen her horse, then she was the innocent here. He quickly finished his search and stepped back.

"Looks legit," Dillon announced. "The papers are notarized and look like the bills of sale I've got at home. On the surface, I'd say that he's telling the truth. Wilkerson owns the stallion, and that last paper clearly states that Palmer is his representative to take care of the horse."

"Since I would never, ever sell Gladiator, those papers are obviously fake." Piper reached into her jacket and pulled out a cell phone. "I might not have the pedigree papers with me, but I've got proof that he's been my horse his entire life."

She unlocked her phone and pressed the screen, then held it so that Colby and Dillon could see it. She swiped her fingers across the face, showing an impressive collection of pictures of a young colt transforming into a mature stallion. The same stallion standing in the next stall.

"Those pictures appear to show that you've owned the horse in the past," Colby said. "But that doesn't prove that you didn't sell him and have seller's remorse." He took the papers from Dillon and scanned them. "The stallion was sold four weeks ago?"

"Impossible," she said. "I was out of state when Palmer tricked my ranch manager into believing I'd authorized the sale and that he was taking him somewhere on behalf of Mr. Wilkerson. Old man Wilkerson doesn't even breed horses anymore, so that was obviously a lie. But he wasn't home when one of the ranch hands went over there to verify Palmer's claim. So Billy felt he had no choice but to let Gladiator go. When I found out what had happened, I filed a complaint with the police. But they haven't been able to reach Mr. Wilkerson to straighten things out. They said until they talk to him, there's nothing they can do. I had to track down Gladiator myself. Now that I've found him, I'm not leaving here without him."

"Billy?" Colby asked.

"Billy Abbott. My ranch manager."

"Got it. Where did the alleged sale take place?" Colby handed the papers back to Dillon, who pocketed them.

"At my ranch," Piper said.

"Horse or cattle?"

"Horse. I run a breeding program."

"Thoroughbreds? Racehorses?"

"Some, yes. I also raise exotics—rare or unusual breeds in this part of the world, including draft horses. They're my bread and butter, steady income while we try to produce the next Kentucky Derby champion. But that's like winning the lottery. The last Derby winner our ranch produced was back when my dad ran the place, when I was just a baby." She frowned. "I don't see how any of that matters, though."

"Just getting some background information. You mentioned this Wilkerson guy like you're pretty familiar with him. Is he a friend?"

"I wouldn't call him a friend, no. We wave when we see each other across the fence or on the road. But we don't typically socialize."

"He's your neighbor?"

"Yes. His property abuts mine."

"But he can't be located. He's missing?"

She shook her head. "No, that's one thing that I can't blame on Palmer. Wilkerson hasn't been kidnapped."

Palmer crossed his arms, glaring at her.

She ignored him. "I spoke to the service that mows his grass and looks after his property when he's gone. They said he's on vacation and won't be back for weeks. But they didn't have an address or even a phone number. According to the police, Wilkerson has checked in a few times, so they're not worried about foul play. But he hasn't checked in since Gladiator was stolen, so I haven't had a chance to talk to him."

She waved a hand toward Palmer. "I've never even met this guy before and he shows up when both Wilkerson and I are gone and waves his fake papers around. If that isn't suspicious, I don't know what is. He probably saw Gladiator out in the field, decided he wanted to steal him and randomly chose Wilkerson as a front for his schemes. I bet he's never even met Mr. Wilkerson."

"Wilkerson, my *employer*, paid good money for him. Just because you changed your mind doesn't mean I have to give you back the horse."

The tent flap opened again and Blake strode down the aisle. "Sorry for interrupting. Thank you, Mr. Palmer, Miss Caraway. Your records came back clean." He smiled and handed them back their IDs. "There's a crowd gathering outside, wanting in the tent to prep the horses for the parade," he told Dillon. "I'll hold them back, but the natives are definitely getting restless."

"Understood. Thanks, Blake."

Blake hurried out of the tent and Dillon walked toward the next stall. "How much did Wilkerson allegedly pay for the stallion?" When he reached the stall door and got his first unblocked view of the horse, he let out a low, appreciative whistle. "Friesian?"

"Yes," Palmer and Piper both said.

"He's thicker and taller than other Friesians I've seen."

After giving Palmer a warning glance, Piper responded alone this time, "That's part of why he's so special. Most Friesians are closer to fifteen or sixteen hands tall. Gladiator is seventeen hands and built like a Clydesdale."

"Gorgeous." Dillon's voice sounded wistful, as if he wished he owned the stallion.

"He's a perfect specimen," she said, "heavily sought after as a breeder. Which is why I'd *never* agree to sell. His stud fees pay a large chunk of the expenses on the ranch."

The pride in her voice and the joy on her face as she talked about the horse were enough to convince Colby that all was not as it seemed. The real question was whether Palmer or his boss, Wilkerson, was the bad guy. Then again, maybe both of them were in cahoots.

"You never answered Dillon's question, Mr. Palmer. How much did your employer supposedly pay for Gladiator?"

"Thirty thousand."

Colby stared at him, stunned.

Piper snorted again. "That's not even half of what he's worth. And the money hasn't been wired to my bank account. I haven't received a single dime. That alone proves he's lying."

Palmer shrugged. "That's between you and Wilkerson. Maybe there was a mix-up in the wire transfer.

The account numbers could have been transposed or something. All I know is that he told me it was taken care of and gave me the papers that *you* signed. I'm sure he'll straighten out the financing hiccups."

"I didn't sign anything." Her hands flexed at her sides as if she wanted to strangle him. "You're a horse thief, plain and simple. You should be shot."

"I think you mean hung," Colby said. "I'm pretty sure that's the time-honored punishment for horse thieves."

She appeared to consider his outrageous statement, then nodded sagely. "Works for me. If Destiny doesn't already have a hanging scaffold, I'll be happy to help them build one. I'll even volunteer to pull the trip lever."

Colby grinned, then sobered when he caught Dillon frowning at him.

"Mr. Palmer," Colby said. "Let's assume for a moment that there really is a mix-up at the bank and it will be straightened out. Thirty thousand dollars is a heck of a lot of money to pay for a horse. It's hard to believe that Wilkerson would send such a valuable animal off to a county fair. Why would he do that?"

Palmer's gaze slid away from Colby. "Wilkerson wants to drum up interest in the horse community so he can command a higher stud fee. He told me to tour the stallion at equestrian events for a few months."

"Lexington is about three hours away. Why bring the stallion that far? Even if everyone in Blount County attends the fair, that's only a few thousand people. A lot of them have horses for pleasure, but I doubt anyone around here is in the market for an expensive exotic like Gladiator. So why bring a prize Friesian to Destiny?"

"Good question," Piper chimed in before Palmer could respond. "Gladiator's too big and heavy to win a race. But he's gorgeous enough to win just about any horse show. What's the purse for something like that? Four? Five hundred bucks? Palmer makes the circuit through Tennessee while Wilkerson is out of state, none the wiser. He pockets thousands of dollars that his employer knows nothing about. Assuming Wilkerson really *is* his employer. Sounds like a lucrative scam to me."

Hatred seemed to seethe from every pore as Palmer stared at her. The man who'd screamed in fear of a pocketknife was long gone. Had it all been an act to make her underestimate him until he could get the knife from her? Maybe he'd heard other people outside the tent and thought his shouts would draw them in as potential witnesses to say that Piper was stealing his horse? One thing was certain. Piper had bought his helpless act and didn't appear to see him as a physical threat, in spite of his size. But Colby had dealt with men like him before. And he suspected that Palmer could be an exceedingly dangerous enemy.

"I'm not breaking any laws." Palmer's voice was low and threatening. "I'm doing exactly what Wilkerson asked—getting the word out about his stallion, hyping up interest."

"This is ridiculous. You're such a liar." Piper flicked her hand as if Palmer was a fly buzzing around her head.

Colby shot a worried glance at Dillon. Dillon's

furrowed brow told Colby that he was just as alarmed. He subtly nodded and widened his stance like a boxer preparing to face an opponent in the ring.

Piper waved her hands again, oblivious to the tension building around her. "This lowlife is not taking my horse. I won't allow it. If you, gentlemen, will excuse me, I need to get Gladiator home."

Normally, Colby wouldn't have allowed a suspect, or a witness—whichever category Piper fell into—to shove past him. But he was only too happy to get her out of harm's way and leave Dillon with the task of calming Palmer down. So he moved aside and followed her into the aisle. But that was as far as he was letting her go. He stepped in front of the door to Gladiator's stall so she couldn't open it.

She frowned up at him. "Will you move out of my way?" She bared her teeth in what was presumably supposed to be a smile but looked more like a grimace. "Please?"

"Dillon," he said, without moving out of her way. "Do you have room for one more while we straighten this out? Might take a few days, especially since it's a weekend and no judge would tolerate us interrupting his fishing time. I hear the largemouths are really biting right now."

"A few days?" Piper squeaked. "I'm not going to stay with someone I don't know, cop or not. And certainly not all weekend. I need to get Gladiator home. Now."

"We'll make room," Dillon said, keeping his focus on Palmer. Equal in height and brawn, Dillon could probably hold his own against the other man if it came to it. But Palmer was a good twenty or thirty pounds heavier, beefier in the chest and gut. It wouldn't be a quick fight, or an easy one.

"I already said I'm not staying with you." Piper didn't sound as flippant or confident as she had earlier. Her gaze flicked from Dillon to Palmer, as if she was just beginning to sense the tension around her and how dangerous the situation had become.

"He's not talking about *you* staying with him," Colby said. "He's talking about the horse."

Chapter Three

"What?" Piper stared up at Colby, wide-eyed, the freckles standing out in stark contrast to her suddenly pale face. "What exactly are you saying?"

"Dillon has a horse rescue farm, Harmony's Haven. He can foster Gladiator there until we straighten out who legally owns him."

Dillon was speaking in low tones to Palmer, apparently trying to calm him down. Colby couldn't quite make out the words. When Palmer nodded, Dillon moved back a few feet and pulled out his phone to make a call. Colby could hear him telling his ranch manager, Griffin, to double up some of the smaller horses in the stable and combine two stalls into one that was large enough to safely contain a draft horse.

Palmer snapped to attention. "Now, hold on a minute." He stepped forward.

Dillon swept up the edge of his jacket and tucked it behind his holster, his right hand poised over the grip of his pistol.

Palmer narrowed his eyes at the unspoken threat but moved back, holding his hands up in a placating gesture. "I just want to remind you that I gave you my papers. I've proven that my employer made a deal to buy that horse. And Caraway's ranch manager turned him over to me. We have a binding contract. There's no need to take my horse."

Piper stood on her tiptoes and leaned to the side to see around Colby. "He's not your horse. You tricked Billy. He knows how important Gladiator is to the future of my business. He's the last horse I'd sell, no matter how hard times get."

"Are times hard right now?" Colby watched her closely.

A light flush colored her cheeks. "We've had a few…problems lately. Nothing we can't weather. But they've taken their toll. That's why I was out of town when Gladiator was *stolen*. I was selling some horses at an auction near Murfreesboro to try to raise enough cash to get us through a rough spot. Unfortunately, I was at the auction when Billy called me and didn't hear my phone. By the time I got his message, Gladiator was long gone. But that all goes to prove my point. If I was going to sell him to raise funds, I'd have taken *him* to the auction. Or I'd have brought him upstate, where there's a better market for Friesians and he'd bring a higher price."

"That doesn't prove anything," Palmer insisted. "You didn't have to take him to an auction because you'd already sold him to Wilkerson."

Piper looked ready to explode after that comment. She opened her mouth to reply but Colby held up his hands to stop her.

"Obviously this isn't something we're going to straighten out with a conversation. You both need to chill and go to the police station on Monday so we can talk to the judge and figure out the next steps."

Piper shook her head. "You're making a huge mistake."

"I'm sorry you feel that way. But I assure you that the horse will be well taken care of in his temporary home at Dillon's place. You don't have to worry about him."

She glanced toward the next stall, her eyes suspiciously bright. Then she looked at Dillon.

"You're the boss here, right? Are you okay with all of this?"

He smiled sadly. "I'm really sorry, Miss Caraway. I can tell you're a fellow horse lover and hate to leave without your stallion. And if we could settle this just by bothering a judge on a weekend, I wouldn't hesitate to do exactly that. But all of the courts are closed. There's no way to verify the ownership records and make a ruling. We have to wait until Monday."

Colby moved to the side, leaving the door to Gladiator's stall unblocked. "You can say goodbye if you want."

Her mouth compressed into a hard line. "I'll say my goodbyes at your friend's rescue farm. I insist on hauling Gladiator in my trailer to make sure he gets there safely. Unfamiliar places make him nervous." She waved at the cut pieces of rope lying on the ground. "That's why Palmer tied him up. Gladiator was probably terrified and caused a ruckus."

Colby waited until she looked at him again. "If I lead the way to Dillon's place in my truck, can I trust you to follow behind, not try to take off and make me chase you down?"

"Of course. It's not like I could win a race towing a nearly two-ton animal behind me. I wouldn't even try. It would endanger Gladiator." She waved toward the rear of the tent. "My rig's out back. A blue Ford F-350 pickup with a custom trailer. *Caraway Ranch* is written on the side."

"All right. We'll load him up in a few minutes. Dillon, you can let Griffin know that he doesn't need to bring a trailer over here. We'll meet him at the stables."

Dillon nodded and pulled out his phone to send a text.

"Wait a minute," Palmer said. "You should load him in *my* trailer. I can settle him in at the rescue place."

"No need," Colby said. "Transportation's already arranged. But thank you for your generous offer."

Palmer clenched his hands into fists. Dillon put his phone away and did the same. The message was clear. His adversary pursed his lips, obviously annoyed, but he relaxed his hands.

"I'll wait outside," Piper said. "I'll load Gladiator after you're finished with *him*." She waved toward Palmer as if he was something that should be mucked out of a stall. Then she turned to leave.

Colby blocked her way again. "Hold it."

She looked up in question.

He held out his hand, palm up. "Keys."

"That's not necessary. I'm not leaving here without my horse."

"Of that I have no doubt. That's why I want your keys, to make sure you don't leave *with* your horse until I'm in my truck and you're following me."

She mumbled a few curses beneath her breath as

she dug into her pants pocket. The woman's language could make a sailor blush. She dropped the keys into his palm. "There, happy?"

"Ecstatic. Thank you."

She whirled around and disappeared out the back of the tent.

With Piper out of harm's way, and her keys safely in Colby's pocket, he directed his attention to helping his partner settle things with Palmer. The guy was dangerous, no question. And Colby wasn't about to leave his boss, his friend, without backup. He waved toward the aisle, indicating for Palmer to join him.

Dillon followed Palmer out, keeping a close eye on their potential horse thief as Palmer stopped in front of Colby.

"Let's head out front," Colby said. "I imagine Detective Sullivan has his hands full by now with the other horse owners wanting inside."

Palmer followed Colby out of the tent without offering further resistance. He'd either calmed down now that Piper wasn't insulting him, or he was putting on a good act. Not trusting the man, Colby remained on alert. He wasn't quite Palmer's equal physically, but he wasn't exactly scrawny. He could give the man a decent run for his money and might even win. And it didn't hurt that three other police officers—Blake, Dillon and Donna, who'd only recently returned with Ashley—were now standing a few feet away, armed, with the edges of their jackets tucked behind their holsters.

While Dillon and Colby had been inside the tent, Blake and Donna had both reversed their jackets and were now wearing them with the police insignia and Destiny SWAT across the back. But Donna was content to stand back with Ashley, to keep her and the baby out of potential danger. Dillon nodded his thanks.

Palmer answered more questions while Colby jotted down the information in his smart phone. Once Palmer was on his way to the parking lot, Colby shook his head. "I sure hope Miss Caraway can prove ownership of Gladiator. I'd really like to arrest that guy. There's something smarmy about him."

"Agreed. He gives off some odd vibes. Is it just me or did he cave way too easily on not taking the horse this weekend?"

Colby watched Palmer pull out of his parking space in the big black truck with a massive black trailer behind it but no business name on the sides. "You think he gave in too easily?"

"If I were in his position, I sure wouldn't let my boss's thirty-thousand-dollar stallion go to a stranger's place without insisting a whole lot more forcefully that I be allowed to go, too, and check the place out."

"Like Piper did?"

"Exactly."

Blake chimed in. "If it's her horse, what do you think the odds are that Palmer will show up at the station on Monday?"

"Not good." Dillon grinned. "Which will give us an excuse to hunt the jerk down and throw him in jail."

"I don't get any of this," Blake said. "Her background check came back clean. But so did Palmer's and even the Wilkerson guy's. The sheriff of Meadow County, O'Leary, told me he knows Wilkerson personally. Says the old guy's a cantankerous jerk who cheated on his wife every chance he got and seemed oblivious that everyone knew about it. Then his wife got sick with cancer and it was like a wake-up call. He doted on her but she couldn't be saved. Since her death, he keeps to himself. Divested himself of his business and rarely goes into town. O'Leary said it makes zero sense that Wilkerson would buy a horse, especially a Friesian. The horses he used to raise were Thoroughbreds."

"What about Palmer? Did O'Leary know anything about him?" Colby asked.

"Not personally. Palmer lives in a different county, on the opposite side of Lexington, out of O'Leary's jurisdiction. So he called the sheriff over there and had him search property records. Palmer owns thirty acres and has his own horse business. But it's small potatoes compared to Miss Caraway. She's got a few thousand acres and employs about twenty people."

Colby shook his head. "I agree with O'Leary that Wilkerson isn't likely to be involved. Palmer must have fixated on Gladiator, did his homework and found out that Wilkerson was Piper's neighbor, just like she theorized. Then he used the old man's name on the fraudulent invoice to make it seem legit—after first making sure that Miss Caraway was out of town. Which means he's probably been watching her and planned this whole thing. But if his goal is to steal the horse, why take it to county fairs? He's not keeping a low profile. The risk of getting caught seems pretty high compared to the money he's making off the shows. It just doesn't make sense."

Blake shook his head. "It's a puzzle for sure. I've got the guys back in the office digging up more info, so we should have a better picture come Monday."

Dillon turned around, apparently to check on his wife. She was standing about twenty feet away with Donna and the baby. Ashley was the model of patience, a smile on her face. She was used to the cop life and how it tended to pull her husband away from family outings, even on weekends.

Being a full-time detective, and part-time, pretty much as-needed SWAT officer, was a 24/7 job. That was especially true since they were the only SWAT team for all of Blount County, and even some other nearby counties that lacked the in-depth training that Dillon was always putting his team through. If something really bad was going on anywhere within a couple hours' drive, the entire seven-member SWAT team was usually called in.

"I don't know about you two," Dillon said. "But I'm out of the mood for the fair now. And I'm thinking we should get my daughter out of the cold. I totally misjudged the wind. I don't want her to get another ear infection."

His wife must have agreed, because she had a thick blanket completely covering the stroller now.

Blake straightened, as if a weight had been lifted off his shoulders. He looked eager to get going, proving Colby's suspicion that he didn't want to be at the fair any more than he did.

"If you guys are okay with leaving early," Blake said, "I'll call Max and tell him to put the potatoes on that monster grill of his. We'll have an early lunch instead of a late dinner."

Dillon narrowed his eyes at Blake, as if only just realizing he wasn't excited about being there. Blake had probably just lost points from his leader. Judging by how Blake's shoulders suddenly slumped, he'd probably just realized that he shouldn't have acted so eager to leave.

The poor newbie couldn't win.

Dillon turned back to Colby, effectively dismissing Blake. "I can call the station, see if they can spare someone to come out and escort Miss Caraway and Gladiator to the farm. They'll take her statement and write up the reports, too."

Colby shook his head. "It's not right sending our weekend skeleton staff out here when I've already got this handled. I'm on call anyway. You guys go ahead. I've got this."

A frown wrinkled Dillon's forehead. "Okay, but forget the written reports. Do that Monday. That'll free you up to head over to Max's once you get Gladiator taken care of."

"I said I've got this. Go. All of you. I'll see you later."

"At Max's?" Dillon pressed.

"Depends on how long I'm at the farm." And whether he could find another football game to watch on TV.

Dillon looked ready to argue, but Ashley stepped up beside him. "We've already pushed Colby into going to the fair even though he didn't want to. Don't force him to go to Max's, too. Maybe he's not ready for company just yet."

Colby would have rolled his eyes at her sympathetic look except that it might have hurt her feelings. He loved Ashley like everyone on their team did. But she spent way too much time concerning herself with his love life, or lack of one. As small as the town was, she should already know that his ex was dating someone else. Then again, maybe that's why she was so concerned. Maybe she was worried that he'd heard about his ex and was upset. Man, he couldn't win today any more than Blake could.

Dillon didn't look thrilled about leaving Colby. "You sure you can handle it?"

This time Colby did roll his eyes. "You're not the only one who grew up around horses. My dad still has a sizable herd on his farm and he suckers us kids into helping him out way more often than I'd like to. I may not be the expert that you are but I can certainly load a horse into a trailer. Even a big horse. Now, quit arguing with me and get that beautiful baby of yours out of the cold."

Dillon stepped in close. "I wasn't asking whether you could handle the horse." He kept his voice low so that only Colby could hear him. "I was referring to Miss Caraway and your obvious attraction to her."

Colby stiffened. "She's a witness and a potential perpetrator. I'm sure that I can resist her *siren's call* and do my job. *Sir.*"

Dillon winced. "I had to ask. You were unfocused back there a few times. That can be dangerous, as you well know, when you're on the job."

Still smarting from Dillon's comments, Colby gave him a curt nod, even while he silently acknowledged to himself that he was right. There was something intriguing about Piper that had thrown him off balance more than once. He couldn't remember the last time that had happened, certainly never on the job. The fact that his distraction was obvious enough for Dillon to have noticed smarted worse than the reprimand.

Dillon stepped back. "Thanks for taking care of things. I'll check on the stallion tonight when we get home. See you Monday."

Colby forced a smile for Ashley as the group headed to Dillon's SUV. With all the baby paraphernalia that had to be lugged everywhere they went, Dillon had traded in his coveted red Jeep for a huge sport-utility vehicle. Even though it was cherry red like the Jeep had been, it was still only one step away from a minivan. Colby shuddered at that thought and didn't mind one bit that he'd be heading home alone today. In a truck.

He wasn't ready to trade the single life for a baby stroller, or to say goodbye to his prized 4x4 pickup that was so high it required a step side to climb into it. Still, he had to admit, married life seemed to agree with his friends. Three of his SWAT teammates had succumbed to the love bug. Dillon, Chris and Max were happier now than they'd ever been. Thankfully the other members of the team—Donna, Blake and Randy, who was out of town right now—were just as intent on maintaining the single life as Colby. There was only so much lovesickness a guy could tolerate at work every day.

"Excuse me," a voice called out behind him.

Colby had to jump back to avoid a face full of muzzle. A dappled-gray mare and its rider clopped past him toward the stands where the derby had been earlier. There were a lot more people on this side of the fairgrounds now, milling around and standing in line at the various food vendors to load up on greasy or sugary snacks before the horse show and subsequent race. Horses were being led out of the tent in a chaotic rush.

When it seemed safe to head toward the tent to check on Gladiator and Piper without getting trampled, Colby started that way. A large bay gelding with flashy white stockings and a blaze on its face rushed from the tent, forcing him to hop out of the way again. Its rider jogged beside him, holding the reins. He waved a sheepish apology and Colby waved back.

The sound of pounding hooves had him whirling around, expecting another horse to be charging down on him. But the sound wasn't coming from the direction of the tent.

It was coming from the parking lot.

He turned in time to see an enormous black horse racing through the rows of parked vehicles, its small rider clinging to the withers and long, thick mane as they galloped toward the trees.

It was Piper. On Gladiator. Bareback, without a bridle to steer him.

Colby cursed and looked around. The white stockings on the bay's legs caught his attention. The gelding was a good fifty yards away now. He sprinted after the horse and grabbed the reins from the rider.

"Police emergency. I need to borrow your horse."

He put his foot in the stirrup and vaulted up onto the saddle while the rider was still sputtering in surprise.

"Yah." Colby slapped the reins and squeezed his thighs, sending the bay into a full-out gallop.

Chapter Four

Piper was forced to slow Gladiator to a fast walk so she could safely thread him through nature's obstacle course. Even though many of the trees had lost their leaves for the winter, the pines hadn't, and there were enough evergreen bushes around to make the underbrush thick and cloying. Low branches reached out like spindly fingers to scratch and pull at the horse's thick mane and tail. Piper's own long curls had been tucked down the back of her jacket. But the constant movement kept spilling her hair onto her shoulders, getting in her way.

She shoved one of the curls out of her face and then tightened her hands in Gladiator's mane. If her plan hadn't failed utterly, she'd have had him safely loaded in the trailer by now. When she'd sneaked into the tent earlier this morning, before the fair opened, she'd been shocked to see Gladiator tied to the boards of his stall. She'd wanted to run right in and free him, but she'd forced herself to wait. With only her ranch manager's description to go on, she had to confirm which of the men milling around in the tent was Palmer. Once she'd seen him enter Gladiator's stall, it had taken everything inside her to keep from running in after him right then and there. But his size was a problem. She'd needed a plan. That's when she'd come up with the idea of disabling his vehicle to get him out of the tent. But first, she'd had to figure out which vehicle was his.

Everyone with a horse in the tent had to register, and that included writing down the makes, models and license plates of their trailers. All she'd had to do was mosey over by the registration table, glance at the clipboards, and she had what she needed to find Palmer's truck and trailer. If he'd locked his truck, she'd have slashed his tires. Probably. Maybe. She wasn't in the habit of destroying other people's property, even if they were low-life horse thieves. Thankfully the truck wasn't locked. She'd rummaged in his toolbox and used his own tools and a rubber washer to tamper with his battery connection. Unfortunately, she'd dallied too long, watching the handsome cop, and Palmer had caught her before she'd escaped with Gladiator.

The man had screamed when she'd turned the knife toward him. But it must have been a ruse to confuse her. Because then he'd surprised her by slamming his fist down on her forearm and grabbing the knife.

She frowned. He wasn't anything like he'd seemed at first. There was something beneath the surface, a capacity for cruelty that had the hairs on her arms standing on end. She didn't know how much of what he'd displayed today was an act and what was real. All she knew for sure was that she didn't trust him, and she never wanted to come up against him again.

Now all she needed to do was ride deep into the woods and wait out whatever search might ensue. She should be able to hire a driver to bring a horse trailer to some remote location on the other side of these foothills. Then she could meet him there, load up Gladiator and be gone before the cops—and Palmer—realized what had happened.

But what would she do after that?

She could take Gladiator home to Lexington and fight Palmer and Wilkerson in the courts there. It would be easier to prove her ownership around people who knew her and knew her horse. But the Destiny police had ordered her to wait for a judge's decree. By going against that order, how much trouble could she be in? Was stealing your own horse even a crime?

Clenching her hand tighter in Gladiator's mane, she used the pressure of her thighs to steer him around a rotten tree stump. He pranced sideways, snorting in agitation.

"Hush now. It's okay, boy. We'll figure a way out of this. Don't you worry."

She urged him across the road and signaled him to stop in front of a deep ditch so she could figure out where they could safely enter the thick woods on the other side. Path chosen, she angled him a few feet farther down the road, then balanced her weight forward to make it easier for him to jump.

A loud click sounded behind her.

"Jump the ditch, and I'll shoot that horse right out from under you," a man's voice called out.

She looked over her shoulder. On the other side of the road, at the edge of the tree line, was Detective Colby Vale, sitting on top of a beautiful bay gelding.

But it wasn't the horse that drew her attention or even the angry expression on Colby's face.

It was the ominous-looking pistol in his right hand, aimed at her mount.

"You wouldn't shoot a horse," she said. "That would be cruel. And mean."

He shrugged. "Maybe I'm a cruel, mean guy. You willing to bet the life of your horse to find out?"

She thought about everything he'd done since the moment she'd met him. He'd been polite, even when she wasn't. He'd been nice and, above all, fair. He was bluffing. Had to be. No way was he the type of man who could kill an innocent animal.

Her hands tightened in the mane. She turned back toward the ditch, ready to send Gladiator bounding to the other side.

"He's a beautiful animal," Colby taunted. "You sure you want to do this?"

She hesitated. He wouldn't shoot. Would he? She'd seen his eyes earlier, admiring Gladiator. And for him to have ridden that bay after her, without her hearing him, meant he knew his way around horses. He knew how to guide them on a trail and keep them quiet. Only someone well-acquainted with horses could do that. And someone that comfortable around horses could never do the horrible thing he was threatening to do.

Could he?

Palmer was familiar with horses. And Piper couldn't imagine him hesitating for one second if he had to kill a horse to get what he wanted.

Her shoulders slumped. "Fine, you win." Sighing

heavily, she pressed a knee against Gladiator's side and turned him around.

Colby threw his leg over the saddle and jumped to the ground. "Walk him toward me. Slowly."

She grudgingly squeezed both legs and Gladiator obediently started forward. "He really is my horse. This is all a huge misunderstanding."

"Which can be straightened out in front of a judge. You shouldn't have run. You've only made things worse."

"And *you* shouldn't have—look out!"

Colby jerked around. The man Piper had just seen hiding in the shadows brought the butt of his pistol down on the back of Colby's head. He collapsed to the ground like a popped balloon.

Piper kneed Gladiator to send him galloping down the road for help. Rough hands grabbed her around the waist, plucking her from the horse's back. Gladiator trotted down the road without a rider as Piper twisted and kicked out with her legs, suspended in midair.

"Let me go!" she yelled, trying to look over her shoulder to see who was holding her. She sucked in a breath when she saw Palmer's face. The cruelty she'd only sensed before was now on full display in the tilt of his grinning lips.

"You want me to let you go? No problem." He opened his hands.

She dropped to the road like a rock, her hands skidding across the asphalt, her right hip bearing the brunt of the fall. She rolled to her side, gasping at the pain that rocketed up her spine. Her hands throbbed like they were on fire, the skin scraped off, leaving them bloody and raw.

Palmer crouched over her. "You know the saying." Laughter was heavy in his voice. "Careful what you wish for."

He slammed his fist into the side of her jaw.

PIPER'S JAW ACHED. Her hands throbbed. Electricity seemed to jolt up her hip and spine every time she moved. But her aches and pains were nothing compared to what was going on with Colby.

He still hadn't woken up from where one of Palmer's henchmen had so brutally hit him with his pistol. His pulse seemed far too fast to Piper, his breaths too shallow.

She cradled his head in her lap, her back braced against the cold metal in the back of the small truck that looked like a million other trucks the average guy might rent to move into a new apartment or a small house. But instead of holding chairs and a table, or stacks of boxes, this one held only her and Colby. And it was currently parked in the woods.

Palmer was on his cell phone on the other side of the clearing, standing by Piper's truck and trailer. He must have had one of his men steal it from the fairgrounds after he'd captured her and Colby. Why he'd steal a vehicle when he had his own was a mystery. Unless the black truck and trailer had been stolen too and he'd decide to ditch them.

Regardless, now both Gladiator and the bay that Colby had been riding were loaded into her trailer. But they might as well have been miles away for all

the good that did. She was even less close to bringing
Gladiator home now than she'd been at the fairgrounds.

There were three men with Palmer. One she'd only
heard and hadn't seen. He was the driver of the truck
that she and Colby were inside. Another was sitting in
the driver's seat of her pickup. The other stood about
fifteen feet away from the opening to the back of the
truck she was in, arms crossed, watching her. He was
the same man who'd brutally knocked Colby unconscious. The same man who'd dumped Colby's body into
the back of the truck as if he were a sack of garbage.

Piper winced at the memory. There were goose-egg-
size bumps on both sides of Colby's head now. And de-
spite her best efforts to apply pressure, the laceration
on the right side of his scalp kept bleeding.

Trying not to be too obvious about it, she glanced
around to get her bearings. They'd been driving for
about an hour, give or take. It was impossible to know
for sure without her cell phone and watch, both of
which had been taken from her.

Even in winter, the pine tree branches were thick
with needles and blocked out most of the sunlight overhead. Piper couldn't tell which way was east and which
was west. So even if Colby woke up and they could
figure out a way to escape, where would they go? One
wrong turn could send them deeper into the woods,
hopelessly lost. This time of year, they'd probably die
from exposure.

Colby groaned, his legs shifting restlessly. His eyes
were still shut. Was he waking up? He was definitely
in pain, judging by the way he kept wincing and pushing with his feet.

The man who was watching them headed toward Palmer. Piper had a feeling that was a bad thing.

Colby groaned again.

"Shh, hush. It's okay," she said even though it wasn't. She smoothed a hand down the side of his face, gently petting his neck like she would have done if he were Gladiator. He settled, responding to her whispered words and gentle touch. She couldn't help smiling. Who knew that a grown man could be comforted just like a horse? She had a feeling that Colby wouldn't appreciate the comparison.

"Is he awake?"

She jerked her head up, her smile dying a quick death. Palmer stood just outside the opening at the back of the truck. She tightened her arms protectively around the wounded man in her care.

"No. He's restless because he's in pain. He needs a doctor. Head wounds are dangerous. You need to take us to—"

"No doctors. No hospitals. Now, get over here so I don't have to shout."

Bristling at the idea of leaving Colby alone, she hesitated.

"Do it now or I shoot your new friend." His hand dropped to the pistol openly strapped on his hip.

She reluctantly lifted Colby's head from her lap and scooted out from beneath him, gently lowering him to rest against the grooved metal floor.

He winced again, and she whispered an apology, even as she straightened and walked to the truck opening. Her hands, her hip, everything throbbed in rhythm with her pulse. But she did her best to push thoughts of her injuries out of her mind and to focus on the man standing in front of her, the height of the truck making them just about at eye level now.

Given the violence that Palmer had already dealt to both her and Colby, she knew they were lucky to still be alive. Prodding his temper didn't seem like a good plan, so she did as she was told and tried not to let her hatred for him show in her posture or the way she looked at him.

"Has he said anything?" Palmer asked.

"No. He's still unconscious."

"You sure about that? My guy said he heard him say something."

She flashed a look of irritation at the man standing a few yards behind him. "Detective Vale *groaned*. I wouldn't call that *saying* something."

He chuckled. "Feisty, aren't you? Just like your horse."

She glanced toward the graceful arch of Gladiator's neck and clenched her fists against her thighs. "What's so important to you and Wilkerson about *my* horse? He could have bought another Friesian somewhere else. Why steal mine?"

He shook his head as if he thought she was crazy. "Haven't you figured it out yet, stupid girl?"

He suddenly grabbed her jaw in a crushing grip. His fingers bit into the bruised flesh, making tears of pain start at the backs of her eyes. She clawed at him, desperately trying to get him to let her go. He did. But then he grabbed her wrists and shook her so hard that her head started throbbing along with everything else in her pain-racked body.

Unbidden, tears tracked down her face. Her cheeks flushed hot with humiliation.

His eyes were as black as she imagined the devil's would be as he pulled her close. A cruel smile twisted his lips. Then he suddenly gave her a brutal shove, sending her crashing to the floor of the truck.

Her right shoulder slammed against one of the ridges in the floor. The pain was intense, immediate, white-hot lava rippling across her nerve endings. The bitter taste of blood filled her mouth as she clamped down on her lips, refusing to allow any noise to escape.

Even though she wanted to sit up in mute defiance, she couldn't. The pain was overwhelming, raw, debilitating. If she moved, if she opened her mouth the tiniest bit, nothing would emerge but screams. And once she started, she might never stop.

His cruel laughter echoed through the hollow confines of the truck as he reached for the rolling door overhead.

"Caraway?"

She blinked, desperately trying to focus through the pain, to face whatever else he was going to dish out. She wanted to scramble to Colby, throw herself on top of him, to protect him. But it was beyond her abilities at the moment to even straighten her throbbing arm from the awkward angle in which it had landed.

His smile faded, and in its place was a look of such loathing that she couldn't help but cringe against the back of the truck.

"Spoiled little rich girl, always too good for everyone else. You don't have a clue who I am, do you?" Spittle flew from his lips as he hurled the words at her like daggers. His knuckles whitened around the rolled-up door overhead.

Spoiled little rich girl? What was he talking about? She'd never been rich in her life. The land was heavily mortgaged because her father had used the equity like a bank, taking out loans against it whenever he needed an influx of cash. She was trying to be more fiscally responsible than her father had been. But it was slow going and at times she was barely able to keep the business afloat.

Wait. He'd asked if she had a clue who he was. She knew him? No. She'd never seen him before. Had she? Nothing about his profile was familiar. Nothing. Not his voice, not his huge, hulking build, not even his soulless eyes. Was this a case of mistaken identity? What did he think that she'd done to him?

He glared at her, his evil eyes making promises that had her wishing she could die right then rather than face whatever torture he had planned.

"Poor little Piper Ann. You still don't get it. Listen up, daddy's girl. *It was never about the horse.*"

The door slammed down, leaving her and Colby in utter darkness.

Chapter Five

Pain. It was Colby's whole world. Surrounding him. Curling and rocking through every joint. But mostly, it pounded through his head, as if someone was hitting his skull with a hammer. From the inside.

Nausea coiled in his stomach. Where was he? What was happening? The last thing he remembered was sitting on top of a bay ordering...someone... Piper? Yes, the woman with the beautiful green eyes and the adorably sassy mouth. That was her name. Piper. Piper Caraway. He'd ordered her to... What? She was on a black stallion. She was... Yes, that was it. She was stealing the Friesian stallion that may or may not have been hers. He'd ordered her to turn the horse around. Then what? Nothing. Nothing but darkness. And pain.

His eyelids were sandpapery, heavy. It took an extreme force of will to open them. He blinked, recoiling against the darkness surrounding him. He couldn't see anything. Was he blind?

"Shh, it's okay."

He froze at the sound of the woman's voice. Piper's voice, above him. While the rest of his body was cold and uncomfortable, lying on hard, unforgiving ridges, his head was cradled in a soft, very warm lap. He tried to lift his head, then groaned at the renewed pounding in his skull.

"Easy now," she whispered again. One of her hands feathered through his hair. She patted his head and idly ran her fingers down the side of his face, all while whispering "It's okay" and "Settle down, boy, settle down."

Settle down? *Boy?*

"You do know that I'm not a horse, right?"

Her hand stilled on his cheek. "You're awake?"

He blinked again. No use. He couldn't see anything. "I think so. Where are we? I can't see a dang thing. Why is my head on your lap? And why are you…petting me?"

A strangled laugh sounded above him and she jerked her hands away. "Sorry. I thought you were still unconscious. I was trying to, um, soothe you. It's dark in here, that's why you can't see."

Her reassurances about the darkness staved off the growing panic about possibly being blind. But the loss of the warmth of her hands almost made him groan again. Perhaps there was something to that "soothing" after all. He lifted his head, gritting his teeth against the pain racking his entire body.

"Easy. I mean, be careful." Her hands gently but firmly pushed against his shoulders, helping him to sit up. "Take it slow. I think you may have a concussion."

No "may" about it. He could feel the world spinning around even though he couldn't see it. Whatever had happened to them was bad. And it was still happening. He needed to figure this out, fast, and protect her. Lying around wasn't going to help either of them.

He braced his hands flat against the floor on either side of him to keep from falling over. Only it wasn't a floor. It was cold and hard, with metallic grooves. The muted sound of an engine carried to him, echoing around them. Everything seemed to be bouncing, moving.

"We're in a truck?"

"A small moving truck, maybe a twelve-footer, like you'd rent to move into a dorm. We're sitting near the cab. The door rolls up and it's locked. Trust me. I tried to raise it."

"Who—"

"Palmer, along with three thugs. Palmer's carrying a pistol on his hip. I've seen the others with rifles but at least one of them has a pistol since he used it to knock you out. He's the one who threw you in here. He and Palmer are driving this truck. The other two are driving my rig. Gladiator and the horse you stole are in the back."

"I didn't steal him. I borrowed him."

"I'm sure that makes the owner feel reassured, especially right now, not knowing where his horse is or whether he's okay."

A twinge of guilt shot through him. But there was nothing he could do about the horse or its owner right now. "You're right. But this…scenario, isn't exactly something I anticipated. Any idea why they're driving your trailer instead of his? Or where they're taking us?"

"I'm thinking his was stolen and he ditched it for mine. As for the rest, some things he said make me think he believes I did something to him. He called me 'spoiled little rich girl,' which I assure you I've never been. The ranch has been handed down for generations. But it's never come with money. It's always been a struggle to hold on to it."

"Then he's mistaken you for someone else?"

"I don't think so. I did at first, but now I'm not sure. He called me daddy's girl and Piper Ann, both of which my daddy used to call me. How could he know that if he didn't know me?"

Listening and thinking seemed to be making his nausea worse. But he had to muddle through, figure out what was happening and make a plan before their captors stopped the truck.

The truck hit a hard bump and Colby could hear her suck in a sharp breath.

"You okay? Are you hurt?"

She let out a strangled laugh. "It's a little worse than that. We've been bumping around back here for a couple of hours. If we don't stop soon, it's going to get messy. My bladder is about to burst."

He smiled in the darkness. His own situation wasn't much better. He stretched his shoulders, trying to work out the stiffness. Now that he was sitting up, the pounding in his head had dulled to a low throb. He reached up to touch the left side, which was the source of most of the pain. As soon as he touched it, a lightning bolt seemed to shoot down the back of his neck. He stiffened, and suddenly two warm hands were pressing against his chest, then running across his shoulders to his hands, pulling them down.

"Don't," she urged. "You got hit pretty hard. I had

the devil of a time stopping the bleeding." A pause, then she asked, "It's not bleeding again is it?"

Her hands slid up his arms as if to find his head, but this time he captured them in his to stop her. The warmth and softness of her touch had fired across his nerve endings, sending blood racing through his veins and igniting a whole new cacophony of pain as his whole body seemed to come alive, aware. Had he been unfocused around her before? Because now, he was completely focused. On her. All he could think about was her soft hands, and the pleasure-pain of having them slide over his body.

Piper Caraway was a very dangerous woman.

"Colby? Are you okay?"

No. He let out a shaky breath. "I'm…fine. My head isn't bleeding." At least he didn't think so. At this point, he didn't really care. He just wanted to get his breathing back under control before she realized her effect on him. Normally he was more disciplined than this. It must be the concussion. He was thinking crazy thoughts. Thoughts that were incredibly inappropriate given their situation.

"Oh, well, good." She tugged her hands from his.

He had to force himself not to reach for her again. How insane was that? Just how hard had Palmer's thug hit him?

"You didn't really answer my earlier question." He was desperate to tilt his world back on an even keel, to assess their situation. "Are you okay? Did Palmer or his men…do anything…to you?"

When she didn't answer, he leaned closer until he

could feel the delicious warmth of her skin radiating out. He cleared his tight throat. "Are you all right, Piper?"

He must have startled her because she jumped, her thigh hitting his. "A little, um, chilly, but otherwise fine."

There was a lightness to her voice that made it sound like she was amused about something. He had no clue what. But she'd said she was chilly, and he didn't want her to be cold. So even though touching her with his thoughts so scattered was about as dangerous as touching a match to a powder keg, he reached out to pull her close and offer her his body heat. When his hands settled around her *bare* waist, he froze. His mouth went as dry as dust.

"Piper?" he croaked, then coughed to clear his throat. "Are you...naked?"

This time she did laugh, a joyful, robust sound that was so rich and honest and so unexpected that he couldn't help smiling. Everything about her surprised him. Maybe that was the problem. No one surprised him anymore. The fact that she did had him unbalanced.

"No," she said when she stopped laughing. "But I did sacrifice my shirt for the cause."

"The cause?" He raised his hand and touched his scalp more carefully this time, feeling the sticky dried blood. "You mean me? You said you tried to stop the bleeding. You used your shirt?"

"Did I mention the back of this truck is empty except for the two of us? There aren't any first-aid kits lying around. I used my hands at first. But I couldn't get enough even pressure that way. My shirt was the only thing I could think of."

"You could have used *my* shirt."

"And leave an injured man both cold and bleeding? I'm not quite that selfish."

The words sounded flippant, but he detected an underlying hurt in them.

"Where's your jacket?" he asked. "You had one the last I saw."

"Apparently I smart-mouthed Palmer one too many times. He pulled over to check on us and I might have called him a few names. He took my jacket in retaliation. Leaving me to shiver in my bra and jeans was my punishment."

Colby immediately shrugged out of his jacket, then tried to settle it around her shoulders.

She jerked back. "What are you doing?"

"You gave up your shirt for me. The least I can do is give up my jacket. I've got a thick flannel shirt on. I'll be fine."

"You're wounded. I'm not taking your jacket."

The sound of the engine subtly changed. Brakes squealed. The truck slowed. Colby braced himself against the back wall as the truck came to a stop.

They were both silent. The sound of voices carried to them from the cab. The driver's door popped open, then the passenger door. Shoes crunched on dried leaves, coming toward the back of the truck.

"We're about to have company." Colby found her in the dark and pressed his jacket around her shoulders. "You want to face Palmer and his men again with or without a shirt? Your choice."

She grabbed the jacket and he could hear the water-proof fabric rustling as she shrugged her arms into the sleeves.

A quick check at his waist confirmed what he'd already assumed. His gun, holster, everything he could have used as weapons or to contact his team were gone.

As the lock rattled at the back, he checked one more hiding place, his right boot. He slid his fingers inside the top edge. The cold handle of his hunting knife was still nestled in the built-in sheath. He wasn't completely defenseless after all.

But bringing a knife to a gunfight wasn't the best plan. It was the last resort of a desperate man. And he wasn't desperate. Not yet. He needed to assess their situation before he showed all his cards.

He jerked his hand back, leaving the knife in his boot as the door was shoved upward. It slammed into the slot in the roof, bouncing against the top before settling.

Colby moved in front of Piper, shielding her from view. But her sharp intake of breath told him she'd leaned around him and saw what he was seeing—three rifles pointed directly at them.

Palmer stood in the middle with the pistol that Piper had mentioned holstered at his waist. The other three thugs looked like they were eager to pull the triggers on their rifles. All they were waiting for was their boss's okay.

"What do you want?" Colby demanded, using his sternest cop voice.

Palmer motioned for the man on his right to move back. "What I *want* is for both of you to get out of the truck. Now."

Chapter Six

Colby stood beside Piper only because she refused to let him stand in front of her. The stubborn woman seemed to think he needed her help to keep from falling. She had one arm around his waist and her shoulder was snugged up beneath his armpit.

Judging by the grins on Palmer's men, they thought he was near collapse, too. Fine. If everyone believed that he had one foot in the grave, then he'd do whatever he could to reinforce that image. Being underestimated by one's enemies, especially when they had guns and he didn't, was an advantage. And he and this brave woman beside him could use every advantage they could get.

He wobbled on purpose. Piper gave him a worried look and tightened her arm around his waist. He gave her a slight smile, trying to let her know that he was faking his weakness without warning the others. But he had no way of knowing whether she understood.

In the truck he'd been bounced around and nauseated. Now that he was standing on solid ground, his stomach had settled and his mind was clear. Adrenaline pumped through his body, erasing the weakness and numbing the pain. Now all he had to do was figure out how to disarm four gunmen without getting Piper or himself killed.

No problem.

He almost laughed at the absurdity and hopelessness of the situation, which made him realize that his bruised brain wasn't thinking quite as rationally as he'd believed.

Palmer said something low to the man on his right, a short young wiry guy who either shaved his head on purpose or had inherited really bad genes. To the uneducated observer, bald-guy didn't appear to be much of a threat. But Colby had many years of law enforcement behind him. Baldy was the type of miscreant who made Colby extremely nervous. He was too calm, too still, too bored looking. And the prison-tat teardrops on both of his cheeks told a frightening story. He'd killed before, at least twice. He probably wouldn't even blink at murdering a cop and a woman.

Bald-guy nodded in response to whatever Palmer had told him. He lowered his rifle and headed to the cab of the pickup that was towing the trailer. Piper's rig was parked directly in front of the moving truck. And although Colby couldn't see the driver's door from where he stood, the distinct sound of it opening, then slamming shut, told him that the man had just gotten inside. The question was why?

He could feel Piper tense beside him, probably wondering the same thing and worrying about her horse.

As if in answer, Palmer approached the remaining two men, who were only slightly less threatening looking than the first had been. One of them had tattoos. The other didn't. Both held their rifles steady. But neither of them seemed to have the same poise, the same eerie stillness their counterpart had. Still, Colby didn't doubt for a second that they'd pull the trigger if ordered to do so. And they wouldn't think twice about it.

After whispering to his men and waiting for their answering nods, Palmer straightened and looked at Piper, then Colby. "Take off your boots. Both of you."

"Over here," Piper told Colby. "There's a log. We can sit there and I'll help you."

He tightened his arm around her shoulders, stopping her as he addressed Palmer. "Why do you want us to take off our shoes?"

The rifle that had been pointing at Piper swung toward Colby.

"This isn't a negotiation," Palmer said.

Piper gave Colby a pleading look. "Come on. It's not worth arguing over."

He disagreed, especially since his knife was hidden inside his right boot. That knife might not be much of a chance, but it could be their *only* chance.

Seeing no way around it, he hobbled and stumbled his way to the fallen log. Piper crouched in front of him, her back to the gunmen as she tugged off his left boot. He made a show of leaning down to help her so it wouldn't raise a red flag when he leaned down to help her with the other boot.

When she slid her fingers in the edge of his right boot, he subtly pushed them against the hilt of the knife. Her gaze shot to his and without even pausing she smoothly pulled the knife out and shoved it into the front pocket of his jacket that she was wearing. He couldn't help but be impressed.

"Hurry up," Palmer called out from behind her.

She yanked Colby's boot off, gave him a lingering look, then turned around and set it down beside the first one. A few minutes later, both of them stood barefoot except for their socks. But even thick winter socks couldn't protect them from the cold. Colby's toes were already tingling and burning. From the way Piper was shifting her feet, she wasn't doing any better.

Palmer held both pairs of shoes down by his side while his men kept their rifles trained on Colby and Piper.

"This is where we say goodbye." Palmer sounded almost nostalgic.

Colby glanced at Piper, then rubbed his left hand up and down her arm as if trying to keep her warm. Once again, her intuitiveness impressed him. She subtly shifted her body and he was able to tuck his hand into the pocket where she'd hidden the knife.

"What do you mean?" Colby tried to stall for time. "You can't plan on leaving us here. We'll freeze to death."

"You won't have time to freeze to death. And trying to run away won't get you far either." He shook the boots and grinned at his cleverness.

Both of his men grinned, too. They each had a Mossberg Patriot, great for hunting deer. But that's not what they were hunting today.

Palmer looked at Piper, his smile fading. "Your mom was nice to me when no one else was. She sneaked me some homemade chocolate chip cookies once. I never forgot that. It's way more than my own parents ever did for me."

She frowned. "Who *are* you? How did you know my mom? And my dad? You know he called me Piper Ann. How do you know that?"

He shook his head. "Doesn't matter. I only saw them a couple of times. But they were nice, especially your mom. I just felt, out of respect for her, that I had to say something."

With that, he jogged to the passenger side of the pickup. He tossed the boots in the back, then hopped inside and slammed the door.

Beside him, Colby could sense Piper watching the trailer as it faded in the distance. Her heart was probably breaking watching her beloved horse disappear. But Colby couldn't worry about that. He had to worry about keeping Piper alive.

Palmer's men seemed distracted by the trailer, too, watching it go down the road.

It's now or never.

Colby grabbed the hilt of his knife, whipped it out of Piper's jacket pocket and sent it hurtling at his target in one swift motion. Piper let out a shocked gasp. The hilt of his knife was buried in one of the gunmen's throats. He made a gurgling sound, then sagged to the ground. The second man jerked toward them, his face contorting with shock, then rage.

Colby dived at Piper, pulling her with him behind the fallen log. The crack of a rifle boomed through the clearing. Wood splintered up in a cloud of sawdust and rained down on them.

Boom! Another round plowed into the log, inches

from the tops of their heads. Piper squeaked in terror, her whole body shaking beneath Colby. He scrabbled in the dirt, found a rock, threw it off to the right. He peered through a hole in the log and saw the gunman jerk toward the noise. This was their chance. Colby grabbed Piper around the waist and yanked her up and toward the woods. In his peripheral vision he could see the rifle swinging back their way. He shoved Piper down behind a tree and scrambled after her, just as the rifle cracked again. The bullet ricocheted off another tree a few feet away.

"Two more," Colby muttered.

"Two what?" Piper whispered, sounding out of breath.

"Shots left in his magazine." He looked around, twisting back and forth. A short thick piece of branch was a good foot away. Could he make it?

"How do you know how many bullets he has left?"

"His rifle. It comes standard with five in the magazine. I'm sure he's got more ammo, unless he's a complete idiot—which I'm not betting on. But if I can get to him while he's reloading, and he's not very fast—"

She grabbed his upper arm. "He seems fast to me. I'm not letting you do something foolish and risk your life even more because of my stupidity. I never should have tried to steal my own horse. I should have listened to you and we wouldn't be in this—"

Colby clamped his hand over her mouth.

A twig snapped somewhere behind them.

Her eyes widened.

He very slowly pulled his hand down, then held a finger to his lips.

She nodded, her gaze flitting past him.

Another twig snapped. Leaves crunched. The gunman was closer now, much closer. Colby glanced around, weighing their options. They hadn't made it very far into the woods. The tree they were hiding behind was the only one thick enough to hide them. It didn't take a genius to figure out where they must be. Most of the other trees were too small to provide good cover.

But if he and Piper stayed put, they were as good as dead.

He pointed to his left, since the sounds seemed to be coming from the right, somewhere behind them. Then he pointed to her and held up three fingers. He folded one down.

She shook her head no.

He frowned and nodded yes. Another finger down.

She frowned, obviously not liking his plan. But then she nodded and gathered her legs beneath her, watching him, waiting.

He couldn't reach the piece of wood he'd been eyeing without giving away their location. Instead, he dug into the ground beside him and managed to scoop a handful of half-frozen dirt, his equally frozen fingers screaming at the effort. He listened for something, anything, that would tell him the location of their pursuer.

Crackle. Crunch. Someone had just stepped on some dried leaves.

He glanced at Piper, then tossed the dirt clod to the right while dropping his remaining finger. The rifle cracked, firing toward where Colby had thrown the dirt while Piper took off to the left toward a clump of trees and fallen logs. Colby whirled to his right, just as the rifleman swung his gun toward Piper.

The man's eyes widened in shock to see Colby so close. He swung the gun back toward Colby. Colby lunged at him, crashing down on top of the gunman and landing with a teeth-rattling thud on the frozen ground.

The rifle skittered away. Colby reared back and slammed his fist toward the other man's jaw. But the man twisted sideways and Colby's fist grazed off his shoulder, throwing him off balance.

The man scrambled away on all fours. Colby swore when he saw how close the rifle was. He shoved himself up and after the other man, jumping on him as the man grabbed the gun.

Boom!

The fifth shot in the magazine whined harmlessly overhead.

The man swore and shoved the rifle, throwing Colby off balance again. He fell onto his back, blinking to try to make everything focus. His head was throbbing and nausea coiled in his stomach. The blood loss and earlier hits he'd taken to the head were catching up to him, making him sluggish, slowing his reactions. Or it might have been the cold or the combination of the two.

Either way, he was in serious trouble.

He shook his head, desperately trying to make two of everything become one again. His vision suddenly cleared. His prey was reaching for a rifle. Not the empty one. The one with a full magazine. The one that belonged to the dead man.

Colby scrambled to his feet, forcing his legs to move

even though the world was still spinning around him. He made it to the cover of trees and kept going. A crashing noise sounded behind him. The gunman was in the woods, too, not far behind. Colby zigzagged from tree to tree as wild shots pinged against the bark or hit bushes inches from him. All he could think about was luring the man in deeper, away from wherever Piper was hiding.

He lurched around another tree and peered around the other side. The rifleman had stopped a good ten yards back and was listening intently. He must not have seen Colby in the deep gloom. The sunlight was having a hard time reaching him through the thick branches overhead and the darkness was providing him cover.

The gunman cursed, then sprinted back toward the clearing.

"Where's he going?"

The whisper had Colby whirling around in surprise to see Piper, hiding behind a tree ten feet away. The realization that he'd led the gunman toward her, instead of away from her, had his insides going as cold as his throbbing feet and hands.

The sound of an engine erupted from the clearing.

"The truck," they both said at the same time.

Colby took off in a wobbly run. He couldn't let the man take the moving truck. It was their only way out. He raced into the clearing, then skidded to a halt, catching himself against the same log where he and Piper had hidden just a few minutes earlier. Taillights disappeared around a curve as the sound of the engine faded in the distance.

He slid to his knees and punched his fists against

the ground. He knew what this meant. It didn't matter that the gunman hadn't shot them. By abandoning them in these woods, he and Piper were as good as dead.

"Colby?"

He squeezed his eyes shut, breathing deeply as he struggled for control. When he felt more composed, he looked up. The raw fear in her eyes had him fisting his hands against the ground again and wishing those hands were wrapped around Palmer and his men's necks for hurting her like this.

She rushed forward and dropped to her knees. "Are you okay? He didn't shoot you, did he?"

He shook his head, unable to speak. Once again this woman had surprised him. He thought she was terrified to have been abandoned, stranded in the woods with temperatures that were rapidly dropping into the freezing range. But she wasn't worried for herself. She was worried about him, a cop she'd only met a few hours ago. A cop who'd essentially taken away the one thing she obviously cared most about—her horse. He'd never felt more like a jerk than he did in that moment.

Forcing a smile that he hoped was reassuring, he shook his head. "I'm fine. The bad guy is gone."

She smiled, looking ridiculously relieved. "That's good, right? Now we just have to follow the road..." Her smile faltered. "I don't see a road anywhere. But there has to be one close by, right? They couldn't have made it into these foothills without a road close by. We just have to follow their tracks and find it. Come on, Colby. Get up. We have to get moving or we'll freeze to death. Let's hurry while we've still got half a day of sunlight ahead of us."

He wasn't sure if she believed what she was saying or if she was in denial. But he didn't have the heart to dash her hopes. He'd let her think they were going to make it out of here alive just as long as he could. Maybe she was right and they weren't as far from civilization as he suspected and they *could* make it out of here. But he didn't think so.

The gunman wouldn't have risked leaving them if he thought they could survive. He wouldn't want to face Palmer's rage if Colby and Piper turned up again later, alive. Still, he didn't want to be the one to destroy her hope. And maybe he could borrow a piece of it himself. As long as there was hope, there was life.

"Half a day ahead of us, huh? That might be enough to get out of here. How long do you think we were in the back of the truck?" He took her offered hands, allowing her to help him to his feet. Truth be told, running through the woods had taken its toll. He was far shakier than he would have expected.

She pulled his left arm around her shoulders and put her right arm around his waist. "Just a couple of hours. They didn't seem to be going very fast, probably so they wouldn't attract any attention. They also stopped several times. And I bet they stayed to the back roads to avoid the police. We could still be in Blount County, or just a few counties over. We'll find a way out of here before the sun goes down. Count on it."

He faked a smile and motioned toward the trees. "Now that we've gotten away from Palmer and his thugs, I can't help remembering another urgent situation we were both suffering earlier. I know I'm still suffering, so you have to be, too."

A pretty pink flush colored her cheeks. "Yes, well, I suppose we could both take a few minutes to, ah, regroup. Then meet back here."

"How about five?"

She nodded, then took off in a run to the cover of trees. As soon as she disappeared, he hurried to take care of nature's call himself. Then he rushed over to the dead man on the far side of the clearing. A quick jerk, then a couple of swipes of his blade against the man's jeans and he had a relatively clean knife. He shoved it into his waistband, then eyed the man's shoes and jacket. They were far too small for him, but they might work for—

"Don't even think about it."

He turned to see Piper's pale face, her gaze averted from the man lying on the forest floor.

"I'm not wearing a dead man's clothes. There's blood all over them," she whispered.

"But it's cold out here. Your feet—"

"I don't care. I'd rather freeze to death than wear a dead man's blood. Please. Don't ask me to do it. Just… don't. I *can't*."

He wanted to argue, but the pleading look in her eyes was impossible to resist. He stepped away from the corpse.

"Ready?"

She nodded and they both started off in the direction where the truck had disappeared.

Chapter Seven

Piper stared at the ground as they walked through the woods. She couldn't deny the facts no matter how hard she looked.

They hadn't found a tire track in a very long time. The hard, frozen ground just didn't reveal much.

She rubbed her hands up and down her freezing arms and risked a quick glance up at Colby. As if he could feel her gaze on him, he stopped.

"What's wrong?" His gaze swept her up and down as if searching for injuries. "Did you get cut on a tree branch or something?"

He put his hands on her shoulders, his fingers gently sliding down each sleeve of her jacket, testing for rips. If she'd been the crying type, she'd have been a puddle on the ground by now. When he didn't find any holes in the fabric, he put his hands on her shoulders again.

"Piper? What is it?"

"There aren't any more tire tracks to follow. We're utterly lost. I'm so, so sorry, Colby. I think I've killed us both." A sob burst from her and she covered her face with her hands. So much for not being a crier.

His arms crushed her against him as he rested his cheek on top of her head.

"Shh, it's okay," he whispered. "None of this is your fault. It's okay."

She shamelessly allowed him to comfort her for one long, selfish minute, reveling in the feel of his strong arms around her. If only they could have met some other time. There was no telling what they could have become to each other.

No, that was a useless thought. She had her ranch, the people who depended on her. He had his job, his friends, his roots here in Tennessee, hours from her home. It never could have worked. But it was a nice fantasy, if only for a moment.

Her moment was up far too soon. But at least she'd had one, magical hug to take with her to the grave. She reluctantly pushed out of his arms and took a step back.

"None of this is right. It's my fault that you're out here. And it's definitely my fault that you don't have a jacket. I should have let you put that dead guy's coat on me. It was stupid of me to refuse. But that was my mistake, not yours. And you shouldn't have to pay for it. I'm freezing with a coat on. I can't imagine how miserable *you* must feel without a coat at all."

She reached for the zipper. His hand was suddenly on her hand, his fingers wrapping around hers, stopping her.

"I'm not taking it," he insisted. "And I'm not letting you die of hypothermia by walking around in your bra, as much as I would enjoy the view." He punctuated his statement with a grin and an outrageous wink, just like the one he'd given her in the tent at the fair.

She let out a burst of laughter, then sobered. "I'm serious, Colby."

"You think I'm not?" He stepped closer, until the tips of his toes brushed hers. He wiggled his feet and winked again.

He was standing so close that his chest brushed against her breasts. Even through the jacket she felt that delicious pressure, and her pulse kicked into hyperdrive. Her breathing hitched, and he must have heard it because his teasing smile faded. His gaze dropped to her lips. His nostrils flared like a stallion's scenting a mare. And suddenly his mouth was on hers.

His lips were cold at first, shockingly so. But his breath was warm, so incredibly, deliciously warm. She breathed him in, molded her mouth to his and kissed him back.

He groaned deep in his throat, and then his arm was beneath her bottom, lifting her. She instinctively wrapped her legs around his waist, and he turned, pressing her against a tree while his mouth did crazy, wonderful things to hers.

When his tongue swept inside, she knew that she'd died and gone to heaven. Nothing had ever felt better. Or hotter. It was as if she'd found her very own furnace in the middle of the mountains, and he was igniting her like a flame.

The kiss went on and on until she was whimpering against him, so hot that all she wanted to do was pull off their clothes. She slid her fingers down his face without breaking the kiss. And then she was pulling at her zipper, desperate to get the jacket off.

"No." One word, husky, strained, and then his hands were around her waist, pulling her off him.

She dropped her legs and he stood her up, his body still pressed against hers, which was a good thing because she nearly fell over as soon as her feet touched the cold ground. They were tingling as if a million icy needles were pricking her skin.

"Ouch, ouch." She shifted from foot to foot. "My feet feel like they're burning."

He chuckled and stepped back. "Mine, too. I think we figured out how to get our blood circulating again. What do you think? One kiss every ten minutes? That ought to keep us alive for a while."

He grabbed her hand and pulled her after him through the woods again.

She rushed to keep up, then looked at him in shock. "Are you kidding me? You got me all hot and bothered back there just to get me...hot?"

He grinned. "I wouldn't put it that way exactly. I wanted to keep you from taking off your jacket and did the first thing that came to mind. Taking your jacket off now would defeat the purpose. You'd be freezing cold in a matter of minutes."

All her guilt came flooding back. He didn't have a jacket. He was probably already freezing cold again while she was only half-freezing. She reached for her zipper.

"Don't," he warned without stopping. "If you try to take off your jacket, I'll just kiss you."

She laughed. "That's not exactly a deterrent."

The corner of his mouth quirked up but he kept his

gaze on their surroundings, leading them both around obstacles in their path.

"My point is that I'd just have to distract you, which has the added benefit of warming both of us. But the downside is that we still don't have shelter from this weather. If we're stuck up here without shelter once the sun goes down, we won't have a chance. We need to keep moving."

"But—"

"But nothing. Keep an eye out for a cave or an old shed or barn. There are tons of abandoned structures all over the Smokies, leftovers from a hundred years ago. Finding a dilapidated lean-to could save our lives."

Probably about forty-five minutes later, Colby's fingers slipped from hers and he fell against a tree.

"Colby!" She reached for him, but he pushed her back.

"I'm okay." He shook his head as if to clear it. "Just lost my balance. I'm o-okay." He took off again, decidedly less sure-footed than he'd been before.

She grabbed his right hand, rubbing it between both of hers as they walked. Had he been that pale earlier? A clicking noise sounded. His teeth were chattering. The rapidly dropping temperatures were taking their toll. If she didn't do something fast, he was going to succumb to hypothermia.

She glanced around, desperately scanning the trees for some kind of shelter. Colby swayed again. She put her arm around his waist and knew he was in really bad shape when he didn't complain or insist that he could walk okay on his own.

"Too bad you're not a smoker," she teased. "We sure

could use a lighter right now to start a fire. I don't suppose you were a Boy Scout and know how to start one without any tools?"

He plodded forward without a reply. His eyes were glassy looking now. Even his lips were pale. Dear Lord, what was she going to do? This man was going to die because of her stupid refusal to wear a dead man's coat. She had to warm him up, and there was only one way she could think of to do that right now. She'd take a play from his own playbook.

Up ahead, a stand of oaks was tightly spaced together, forming a semicircle. It wasn't much of a shelter, but it would block some of the cold air. She yanked her hand out of his and pressed him back into the group of trees. Then she yanked the zipper down on her jacket too fast for him to realize what she was about to do. The jacket was off and draped around his shoulders before he could protest.

He didn't protest at all.

Instead he blinked at her, swaying like a drunk as if he was trying to figure out what was happening.

That's when she unsnapped her bra.

If she'd lacked any confidence about her body, she'd have died a quick death of humiliation right then and there. Because all Colby did was sway in the wind, his eyes still glassy. But at least they were open. And his gaze was right where she wanted it.

She flung her bra to the ground, her large breasts tight and perky in the forty- or maybe thirty-degree temp now. Her skin prickled with goose bumps all over and she felt like she was going to die herself if she didn't put the jacket back on. But she wasn't about to get dressed again until Colby was coherent and *demanding* that she put the stupid coat on.

He leaned back against the trees as if he didn't have the strength to stand on his own. But still he said nothing. Did nothing.

Tears clouded her vision. Was she too late to save him?

She blinked the tears away. No time to dwell on her own useless emotions. This was about saving Colby. She stepped between his thighs, her belly pressed against the most intimate part of him through his jeans. Then she lifted his hands, which were ice-cold. She drew a deep breath, bracing herself, then pulled his hands to her breasts.

They both jerked at the contact, him probably from the shock of realizing that her naked breasts were filling his palms. Her because it was like immersing herself into an ice-water bath.

"P-Piper," he whispered through chattering teeth. "Wh-what are…y-y-you—"

"Just touch me," she whispered back, molding his fingers around her breasts, pressing herself against him. "I want you to touch me, Colby." She did a sinful swivel with her hips.

His eyes widened. His tongue darted out to moisten lips that were cracked and dry. And then, finally, his fingers began to move. She closed her eyes and leaned into him, moving her hips, rubbing against him like a cat. His fingers tightened, slid across her skin, testing the weight of her. One of his thumbs brushed her nipple and she had to hold back a moan.

Something about this man set her nerve endings on

fire. She'd started doing this to warm *him* up. But just a few minutes in and *she* was practically sweating. All she could think about was how wonderful he smelled, how wonderful he felt. Especially…there. She swiveled. He sucked in a breath, his body jerking against hers through the fabric of his jeans.

She slid her hands up his shirt and buried her fingers in the wispy ends of his thick dark hair.

"Kiss me," she begged. "Kiss me, Colby."

His head dipped down but his movements were still sluggish, his face far too pale. He didn't take the lead like he'd done before. She stood on her tiptoes to reach him, brushing her lips against his once, twice, before his mouth parted on a soft breath of surrender. This time she swept her tongue inside his mouth, stroking, sucking, coaxing the passion from him, igniting the fire in him that he'd started deep within her.

But this kiss was different. It was slow, tender and so sweet it had her heart melting in her chest. He was kissing her back now, but he was giving more than taking. Cherishing. Loving. Another breath shuddered out of him and he broke the kiss. He pulled back, his eyes focused again.

"What are you doing to me, Piper Caraway?"

"I'm rescuing you, Colby Vale. And I'm not finished yet."

His grin, that gorgeous, sweet, lopsided grin was back. Colby was back. She nearly wept with joy when he slid one of his hands down her back to her bottom and caressed her through her jeans. Then he was lifting her as he'd done before, but this time he didn't stop when they were at eye level. His grin widened as their gazes met, then he lifted her higher and turned her around, pressing her against the trees.

His hot mouth came down around her nipple and she very nearly came undone. She arched her breast against him, her hands clutching his shoulders, breaths gasping out of her so fast she felt dizzy. Then he was lowering her to the forest floor, the jacket suddenly beneath her back, keeping that part of her warm. And Colby was on top of her, making the rest of her *burn*.

His mouth was everywhere—on her belly, her breasts, sliding up her neck and making her arch against him. Then he was doing sinful things to her mouth again. The man knew how to kiss. She could kiss him forever, sink into the forest floor and die a happy woman. But she wanted more, so much more.

Reaching down between them, she grabbed the snap on his jeans.

Suddenly his fingers were like a vise wrapped around her wrist, stopping her.

"Don't," he choked.

Her eyes flew open, and she nearly wept at the concern and want and need etched into his features as his gaze drank her in.

"Why not?" She forced the words from her tight throat. "I want you." She slid her hand down the impressive ridge in his jeans, making him jerk against her. "And you obviously want me. I can't think of a better way to stay warm."

He shuddered and shook his head. "If I'm ever lucky enough to get you into a bed with a box of condoms, I'm not letting you go for a week."

She grinned. "Deal."

He laughed, then sobered. "Piper, if we stay here, if we make love, we'll both end up falling asleep in each other's arms. It's called hypothermia. We'll never wake up again."

She stared up at him, her playfulness forgotten. The heat they'd generated no longer seemed quite so hot. His face was still far too pale. And it dawned on her that he was right. Their judgment, her judgment, was seriously impaired. This might have seemed like a good idea, but it wasn't a solution. Both of them were half-dressed now and getting colder by the second. And she knew he was right. If they fell asleep in each other's arms, that would be the end.

"Then what do we do?" she asked. "I can't wear that jacket all the time and watch you freeze to death in front of me. I don't want to be Rose while Jack dies."

His brow wrinkled. "Rose? Jack?"

She stared at him in horror. "The movie *Titanic*? Leonardo DiCaprio and Kate Winslet?"

His mouth curved in a wicked grin. Then he winked.

She shoved at his shoulder. "You scared me for a second. I don't think I could continue to allow myself to be lost in the woods with a man who'd never seen that movie. It's epic."

"Star Wars or Star Trek?" he asked.

She rolled her eyes. "Dumb question you ask, dumb answer you will receive."

"I knew it." He kissed her, then smoothed her hair back from her face. "You're kind of perfect, you know that? Yoda?"

She grimaced. "Calling me a hairy green man isn't going to get you to second base." She blinked, looked down at their half-naked bodies plastered together. "Um, *home* base I guess I should say."

He laughed and pulled her up, then grabbed the jacket.

"Wait." She held up her hands, refusing to let him put it around her shoulders. "I'm serious about what I said. I'm not wearing the jacket all the time anymore. We have to take turns."

He shook his head and handed her the discarded bra, which she quickly put on.

"I'm not letting you walk through the mountains with only a bra to keep you warm," he insisted.

"Fine. Agreed. Give me your shirt. You take the jacket."

He frowned, but when he would have argued, she put a finger against his lips to stop him.

"I mean it. We take turns with the shirt and the jacket. Maybe a little kissing, too, if that's what it takes. I'm willing to suffer for the sake of survival." She winked at him, making him laugh. "But we share what we have so we can both survive."

He was already shaking his head and trying to put the jacket around her again.

She cursed and swatted it down. "Look at it this way, Colby. If you freeze to death, you're leaving me all by myself up here. And whatever survival skills you have, trust me, I have far less than that. I'm great on a horse ranch. Anything else is beyond me unless I can call room service or a taxi. If you die, I die. So what's it going to be? Are we going to waste all the warmth we just generated arguing? Or do I get your shirt for a while so you can take turns wearing the jacket?"

She could tell it about killed him to agree to her terms. But even he couldn't deny her logic. Either they both survived, or neither of them survived. They had to work together.

Maybe twenty minutes later she was shivering so hard in his flannel shirt that she was doubting her sanity in ever insisting on giving up the jacket. It didn't take much coaxing on Colby's part to talk her into the first switch, giving him back the shirt while she wore the jacket again. But she kept a close eye on him and tried to count the minutes in her head to ensure they both had equal time wearing the jacket.

The downward slope of the mountain started leveling out. It took a few minutes for that new information to sink in. Then it dawned on Piper what it could mean for them. She grabbed Colby's hand.

"It's not as steep anymore. Are we out of the mountains? Maybe there's a road close by now?"

He squeezed her hand and let it go, looking far less excited than she'd expected.

"It's leveling out. But that doesn't mean we're out of the mountains yet. It could just be a plateau." He turned, scanning the trees. Then he pointed. "Over there. See how the trees break and the undergrowth disappears? We should be able to see something from there, maybe get our bearings if nothing else. If the break is large enough, cabins or houses on adjacent slopes might be able to see us and vice versa. We could try to signal for help."

He let her hand go and hurried across the clearing toward the break.

The thought of someone seeing them, or her and

Colby finally seeing some of the houses that had to be scattered throughout these mountains had her clasping her hands together and offering up a quick prayer.

Thirty feet away, Colby stopped at the break. He looked past the opening, then stiffened.

"Piper? About how long did you say we were in the back of that truck?"

She pushed a low-hanging branch out of her way, carefully stepping over a fallen log. "All total, maybe three hours, I'm guessing. And we've been up here two or three more ourselves. It's probably around three in the afternoon, if that. Why?"

He watched her as she stepped into the clearing. The concern on his face had her more worried than ever. He waved his hand toward the vista to her left. She turned, then pressed a hand to her throat.

Spread out before them, in varying shades of reds and golds, was the beginning of one of the most spectacular *sunsets* she had ever seen. It was almost nighttime. The gloom in the forest that she'd attributed to the thick tree cover was actually the sun going down. Which meant they hadn't been in the back of the truck for just a couple of hours.

They'd been driving for most of the day.

She must have fallen asleep and had never realized it. But misjudging the time, not realizing it was close to the end of the day wasn't what concerned her the most. And she knew it wasn't what had lines of concern furrowing Colby's brow either.

It was the endless rows of mountaintops spread out before them. As the sun began to spread its last rays across the land, there wasn't even a hint of light from a nearby business, home or even a forest ranger's cabin. Nothing about the vista looked familiar and she understood why. Palmer hadn't dumped them somewhere in the Smokies. He'd dumped them deeper in the Appalachian Mountain range. Miles from civilization. And they didn't even know which part of the mountain range they were in. They could be anywhere from Tennessee, to the Carolinas or even Virginia. There was no way to know.

The only weapon they had was a knife and they didn't have any supplies. Neither of them had shoes. Colby had a head wound. Temperatures were plummeting and there was only one shirt and one coat between the two of them.

"Well," she muttered. "Look at the bright side."

He slid her a curious glance. "What would that be?"

"Things can't possibly get worse."

A deep rumble sounded overhead.

They both looked up as the first drops of freezing rain landed on their faces.

Chapter Eight

"You had to say it, didn't you? 'Things can't possibly get worse.'" He leaned back against the pine tree beside the one she was leaning against. The canopy was keeping the worst of the rain off them. But they were still soaked, with no hopes of getting dry anytime soon.

"You can't possibly blame me for the rain." She sounded completely outraged.

"Sure I can." It was hard to sound serious when she made him want to laugh.

She narrowed her eyes at him.

He grinned and put his arm around her shoulders, pulling her close. "I'm teasing."

She let out a deep sigh. "We're never making it out of here. I vote that we go ahead with my original plan. Make love. Die happy. What do you say? Should we make like rabbits and have some fun?"

This time he did laugh. "Where have you been all my life?"

"Waiting for you of course."

They both smiled.

"All right," he agreed. "If it gets to the point where we're out of options, we'll do it your way. Make love.

Die happy. *Very* happy." He punctuated his statement with a lusty leer.

She burst out laughing. "Only you, Detective Vale, could make a woman laugh when she's thirsty, starving, freezing and hopelessly lost."

"I can usually make a woman laugh without all those variables. But since you don't have the pre-stranded-in-the-woods Colby to compare me to, I'll count that as a compliment."

"Please do."

A chattering noise sounded above them. He squinted up against the misty rain. "Too bad all I have is a knife. If I had my pistol I'd shoot that squirrel out of the tree and we wouldn't be hungry anymore."

She grimaced. "Raw rat with a bushy tail isn't my idea of a meal. But don't knock the knife. It saved our lives back in that clearing. Who taught you to throw a knife like that?" She rested against the trunk of the tree beside him again, rubbing the sleeves of the jacket as if trying to ward off the cold.

Trying to keep her mind off how wet, cold and miserable they both were, he said, "It's hard to say who taught me to throw a knife. My dad taught all three of us—my brother, sister and me—about guns. I reckon he could be the one who showed us how to throw knives. But it might have been my grandpa instead, or even my mom. I grew up with a knife in my pocket. Can't even remember the first time I tried throwing one."

"I remember my first time," she said. "I was ten. My mom had finally given up on me ever wanting to do the normal girlie extracurricular activities like ballet and cheerleading. So dad took me out in a field with some knives and bales of hay with targets tacked to them to try out his idea of fun. I hit the bull's-eye my very first throw. He said I was a natural."

"Really?"

"Really."

"Huh." He scrubbed his jaw. "Maybe I'll let you throw the knife the next time we run into some bad guys."

She shook her head, her wet hair leaving trails of moisture across the jacket. "No, thank you. I don't think I could ever throw a knife at another human being."

"No matter how bad they are?" he asked, turning serious.

"Even then."

"What about if it was the only way to save someone else's life?"

She hesitated. "I don't know. Let's pray I never have to find out." She gestured toward his boot. "You said you don't remember ever not having a knife. Is that why it was tucked into your boot? Habit? Or is that standard equipment for people who go to fairs in Tennessee?"

"With all the free-flowing beer at those events, I sure hope not. I wouldn't want to come up against a drunk waving a knife around. Honestly, I didn't give it a second thought when my buddies showed up at my house and pressured me into going. I grabbed my work boots since they were by the front door. Having a large knife comes in handy on the job, so I keep it tucked in a sheath inside my boot."

"Handy how? Instead of breaking up bar fights with a billy club, you pull a knife?"

"That might be fun. I should try that next time."

The rain was starting to slack off, and he could see the occasional shiver rack her body. He wasn't doing much better himself. So he motioned for her to get moving and they both headed through the woods again.

"You said you have a sister and a brother?" she asked, her teeth starting to chatter.

He studied her with concern, then took her hand in his, pulling her with him at a faster pace to keep them moving and generating body heat.

"I've got an older sister and a younger brother. And more cousins than I can count. My brother Scott's got a farm not far from my patch of land, just down the road from my mom and dad. Lisa had a thriving estate auction company she'd been building since she graduated *high school*, if you can believe it. She was a real entrepreneur."

"Was?" Her gaze shot to his, her brows crinkled with concern.

"Oh, no, no, nothing like that. She's alive and well. But when she met Joey, everything changed. She sold her business, her house and most of her belongings and moved to Nashville a couple of months ago, all to support her husband's dream of becoming a singer. Now she spends her days saying, 'Do you want fries with that?' and her nights saying, 'Welcome to Walmart.'"

"She sounds like a wonderfully supportive wife."

He snorted. "*Supportive* being the operative word."

"You don't approve?"

"Actually, I do. They're happy. That's what matters. I just wish she didn't live so far away. And that she hadn't given up her own dreams to help her husband chase his. Still, that's her choice. And like I said, she's happy."

"Well, maybe he'll hit it big and they'll be able to afford a home back here and one in Nashville and visit a lot."

He shot her a sideways glance. "The only way Joey's gonna get a record deal is if his audience is deaf."

"Ouch. That bad?"

"Trust me. In my sister's case, love is blind. And hard of hearing."

She shook her head, smiling. "She sounds like someone I'd love to meet. I always wanted a sister. Can't say I ever really wanted a brother, though. God didn't grant the first wish but granted the second."

"No siblings?"

"Nope. But I can't really complain. My parents were wonderful. Overall, I was a really lucky girl to wind up with the family I had. I was blessed. And when they passed, Aunt Helen was just like a second mom. So I guess I was twice blessed."

He squeezed her hand in his. "Sounds like we've both been blessed."

The happiness in her eyes faded and the hollow, empty look that he'd seen in them way too much today was back again. He stopped and pulled her around to face him. She looked up in question, and he couldn't resist gently wiping her horribly matted hair back from her face. The shiver that swept through her body could have been from the cold. But he couldn't help hoping part of it was because she liked his touch.

"I know things are pretty bleak right now," he told her. "And you're probably thinking all our blessings are in the past. But whatever happens, I just want you to know that I'm feeling blessed today."

Her eyes widened. "You must have a fever. You're delirious."

"No, I'm serious," he assured her. "This is the most miserable day, and night, that I've spent in my entire life. But in the midst of all of that, you've made me laugh and smile. I don't know anyone else who could have done that." He cupped her face. "Thank you, Piper Caraway. Meeting you has been a true gift." He pressed a soft kiss against her lips.

A single tear glinted in the moonlight and slid down her cheek as she stared up at him.

He gently wiped it away. "Come on. We have to keep moving."

They trudged across the muddy ground, his arm around her shoulders, hers around his waist, both of them helping each other keep moving. The rain finally stopped. But the damage had been done. Both of them were bone-deep cold and shivering.

How long until dawn? Until they'd be able to stop and soak in the sun's warming rays? Until the temperatures would raise once again and the constant threat of freezing to death would be over? He'd lost all track of time. It seemed like it had been an eternity since they'd begun their trek down this mountain. Was there even a chance now that they could make it long enough to feel the sun on their faces again?

The familiar clicking sound of Piper's teeth chattering had him looking around the woods in frustration.

"There has to be a cave around here somewhere. The Smokies up near Gatlinburg are riddled with them. I don't expect this part of the Appalachians to be all that different. We need to make that our priority. Finding a cave."

"Don't bears use those caves?"

"There's this amazing thing called hibernation during the winter. Ever heard of it?"

Her cheeks, already red from the cold, flushed even redder. "Give my feeble mind a break. I'm not exactly firing on all pistons at the moment."

He *really* hated Palmer and his men right now.

"Change of tactics. Instead of keeping an eye out for caves, let's listen for waterfalls."

She frowned. "Waterfalls? How's that supposed to get us warmed up?"

"The water scoops caves out of the rock. Where there are waterfalls, there are usually caves. Caves mean shelter. Shelter means warmth. Come on. Let's find a waterfall."

Chapter Nine

Colby's tactic of talking to keep Piper from shutting down was running out of steam. He'd told her all about his SWAT team and nearly every funny story from his childhood that he could remember. He was running out of stories and she was asking fewer and fewer questions. It was time to draw her out, make her do the talking.

"Spoiled little rich girl, huh?" He climbed a small boulder to check on a shallow depression above it.

She swayed on her feet below and blinked slowly as if it took more energy than she had left to figure out what he'd just said.

"Spoiled?" she asked. "Wait. Did you just call me spoiled?"

The depression was too shallow for all but the smallest animal to use as shelter, so he jumped back down. He winced when his numb foot came alive at the feel of a sharp twig piercing it. He yanked it out of his soggy sock and threw the stick down.

Piper was looking at him, a hint of curiosity in her dull green eyes. Just enough curiosity to keep her from drifting off into whatever fantasy land she kept disappearing to as they walked along, hunting water-falls and caves like a drunk searching for unicorns and fairy dust.

He took her hand and tugged her forward again. "Palmer called you spoiled, right? That's what you said, that he called you a spoiled little rich girl. Why would anyone think that? Are you sure you aren't rich?"

She snorted, a spontaneous, extremely unladylike snort.

Colby had never heard anything so beautiful. It was proof that the delightful spunky woman he'd met just—what, twelve, fifteen, twenty?—hours ago was still in there somewhere.

"Does that mean yes, of course you're spoiled and rich, or no, you're as poor as a field mouse and as grounded as a hibernating bear?"

She gave him an aggravated look. "M-making fun of my bear f-fears again?"

Her chattering teeth drew her words out, but at least she was talking and making sense.

"Of course not. Still waiting to hear about you being spoiled and rich, though."

"T-told you we were never r-rich. Sp-spoiled in some w-ways, I can buy that, if we're talking about when my p-parents were still alive. But m-money was al-ways t-tight. Daddy put everything he had back into the r-ranch. He said we owed it to the people count-ing on us for a living to make the business our number one priority."

"He sounds like a good man."

"He was. Very. They both were."

"Your mom was a man, too?" He held his hands out in a placating gesture. "No judging. Just asking."

She rolled her eyes. "You need to work on the comedy routine."

He pressed a hand to his chest. "You wound me deeply."

She laughed, a real laugh this time. And her teeth weren't chattering nearly as violently as before. He held up another low-hanging branch so she could duck beneath it.

"How old were you when your parents died and your aunt Helen took you in?"

A faraway look entered her eyes. "Fourteen. They were killed in a car accident. I lost them and my home at the same time. Aunt Helen didn't live in Lexington and refused to move to the ranch. Instead, she hired a guy barely out of high school, Billy Abbott, to manage the business. Thankfully he did a pretty good job because the place is still standing. And he didn't hold it against me when I let him go after taking over the ranch as an adult. I rehired him later on when I realized I needed help with the business end of things." She waved her hand in the air as if clearing away memories. "Anyway, I had to move to Paducah with my aunt, a few hours from the only home I'd ever known. You could say I took it out on her, both my grief and my resentment. Poor Aunt Helen. I was awful, a brat, rebellious." A smile curved her lips. "But she loved me as if I were her own. No matter what I did, she was always there for me. Looking back now, I guess I really was spoiled." Her mouth tightened in a hard line. "That part Palmer got right."

He stepped over a small boulder in their way and lifted her to the other side. She smiled her thanks and trudged through the rain-slick leaves and pine needles littering the ground.

"Piper. What all did Palmer tell you? I remember him talking about your mom and saying that she was nice to him."

"She baked him chocolate chip cookies."

"But you don't remember him?"

"No. When I try to picture him, I come up blank."

"How long ago did your mom pass away?"

She looked down at the ground.

"Piper." He paused and gently tilted her chin up. "It's important. You said you were fourteen. How many years ago was that?"

"You're not supposed to ask a woman her age."

"Piper."

"About ten, okay. Why?" She started forward again and he hurried to catch up.

"I would have been sixteen," he said. "And I figure Palmer is a good three or four years older than me. So he'd be around nineteen or twenty. Did he say he knew you back then? That you ever spoke to each other?"

She shook her head. "He only talked about my mom." She frowned. "The only way I could have known him was if he was at my school or on the ranch. It couldn't have been school since he's so much older. And there weren't any ranch hands named Todd Palmer."

"Maybe that's not his real name. Did your mom work outside the ranch?"

"No. She rarely ever left home. Dad went into town

when they needed supplies. Cooking and cleaning and trying to keep me from killing myself with all my shenanigans was a full-time job for mom."

"So if she met him, it would have been at your home. Think hard. Try to picture him younger, probably slimmer, maybe even gangly. Guys take a while to grow into their frames and fill out. He could have been skinny, which would make him seem even taller than he is now. Dark hair. Maybe he wore it longer." He looked over at her, studied her face. "Anything?"

"No. Sorry. Nothing." She grabbed his hand, her brow furrowed in concentration as she walked. "Wait. He said that kidnapping us was never about the horse. But if it's not about Gladiator, what's it about? The Piper Ann part is really confusing me."

"Confusing how?"

"My middle name isn't Ann. It's Leigh. The only one who ever called me Piper Ann was my father. It was a running joke between my parents because they argued at the hospital over what my middle name should be. Mom felt like Ann was too generic, so she picked Leigh. She liked the uniqueness of spelling it *L-e-i-g-h* instead of *L-e-e*. Said it was special. But for Ann, she said all she could do was maybe add an *e* at the end. They both seem generic to me, but I guess I can see her point." She waved a hand. "The point is that legally my middle name is Leigh. No one ever called me Piper Ann except my father. If Palmer thinks my name is Piper Ann—"

"Then he heard it from your father."

"Exactly. He obviously met both of them, spoke to both of them. Maybe he saw me from a distance and knew I was their daughter, because Dad said something about me and called me Piper Ann. That could have happened. That has to be what happened."

"Did you know all of the people who worked on your ranch? Back when your parents were alive?"

"Absolutely. Mom loved to bake and made cookies and sweet breads for everyone who worked for us. But I was usually the one who'd take them out to the stables or to the barns to hand them out."

"So Palmer didn't work on the ranch."

"I really don't think so."

"But he likely had to have been there, at least a few times to have met your mom, since you said she rarely left the ranch. But he wasn't a regular or he'd have met you and you'd remember him. Thanks, Piper. That helps." He held up a branch for her to pass under.

"I don't see how that helps," she said.

"It gives us some parameters for an investigation. We can focus on your mom mainly, and partly on your dad, which means going back ten-plus years. You'll have to try to remember their routines and where they went. If we can figure out how they could have met Palmer without you meeting him, that might help us figure out the connection between them. And that could help us determine what his motivation is, why it's not about the horse."

She shook her head. "In all this time that we've been out here, I haven't even thought about Gladiator."

He waved his hand at their surroundings. "You've had a few other things to worry about. I think Gladiator would understand."

She laughed bitterly. "We both have plenty of other

things to worry about, for sure. But I hope he and that gelding you took are both okay."

Colby frowned. "If it wasn't about the horse, then why did he go to such trouble to steal your prize Friesian?"

She shrugged. "To get me to follow him? He certainly didn't try to hide the fact that he was traveling the fair circuit. He registered my horse under his real name. He had to know I'd catch up to him eventually. Maybe he wanted me away from the ranch, so he could abduct me?"

He shook his head. "That's a convoluted way to get you alone. Why go to so much trouble? Do you have incredible security that would have prevented him from sneaking onto your land and grabbing you?"

"Not really. I mean, there's a fence, but it's designed to keep horses in, not people out. I hop over it all the time. The house has locks of course, but no alarm. I do have a ranch hand who doubles as a security guard at the stables. His name is Ken Taylor. I hired him a few months ago, after the mishaps started, to ensure that nothing happened to any of the horses."

The fact that she'd hire a security guard to watch over her horses, instead of worrying about her own personal safety, had him mentally swearing. He respected her love for her animals. But the woman needed to learn to put herself first. He drew a steadying breath rather than lecturing her on personal safety. It wasn't his place, and it was a moot point given their current predicament. Instead, he asked, "What kinds of mishaps?"

"Things being misplaced or broken, far more than

usual. It could all be a coincidence. That's what Sheriff O'Leary thinks. He's been out half a dozen times in response to my calls and he's the one who recommended Ken Taylor to me, for peace of mind. But he's never found any evidence of true foul play." She shrugged. "Until this thing with Gladiator, I figured we were just having a bad run of luck that was, unfortunately, hurting our bottom line and causing financial trouble. It's kind of crazy, too. Just three months ago I was planning a major expansion. I was going to add a whole new wing to the stables. Had the plans all drawn up and construction scheduled. Now that's a pipe dream unless I can turn things around."

"Can all of the problems with your ranch be traced to a few months ago?"

Her eyes widened. "I hadn't really thought about the timing before. But yeah, I guess so, pretty much. Right at about two months."

"Hired any new ranch hands in those two months? Someone who might hold a grudge against you?"

She shrugged. "Why would anyone have a grudge? As far as hiring new people, they come and go all the time. About half are long-term employees. But the rest are part-time."

"How many ranch hands do you employ?"

"Twenty or so."

He whistled. "That's a lot of people. You must have a huge ranch."

"Big enough. But the profit margin isn't great these days, so it's not much of a moneymaker. Honestly, I'd probably sell off half the land and downsize the business tremendously to ease the stress of trying to make ends meet if it wasn't for the fact that I employ so many people. I can't just let them go. They need their jobs. They have families to feed. Even the part-timers rely on seasonal work to make ends meet. A lot of them are repeaters, coming back the same months every year."

He smiled, already hearing the lecture his own father would give Piper if he heard her talking that way. Business was business and his dad would say that you had to make tough decisions to keep from going bankrupt. His father wouldn't have thought twice about letting people go and downsizing if that's what would keep the bottom line healthy. His father wasn't unkind or unfeeling. He'd give each person a generous severance package to tide them over until they found new employment. But his reasoning was that he was saving jobs by not risking the entire operation going under. The fact that Piper was too softhearted to do the same wasn't a bad thing in Colby's view. It meant that she was generous and kind, qualities which seemed to be in scarce supply these days.

"Why are you s-smiling?" she asked, a shiver creeping into her voice again.

"No reason," he said, eager to resume the conversation lest she slip back into the near-hypothermic state she'd been in earlier. Switching the shirt and jacket back and forth and briskly moving through the woods while they talked had helped to push back his own chill. But she was much smaller and seemed to be in steady decline. He needed to keep her talking and moving.

"Back to Palmer," he said, pressing his hand against the small of her back as they circled a thick group of pine trees. "If his primary goal was to kidnap you, he could have taken you when you were out in the field or even in town, back in Lexington. Maybe that would have drawn too much attention. Maybe kidnapping you *was* his goal, and by having you leave of your own accord to track down Gladiator, he got his wish."

She slowly nodded, looking thoughtful. "I suppose that makes sense. If I just disappeared, Billy would have called the police. But right now, he thinks I'm still out looking for Gladiator. He has no idea that I'm missing."

"What happens if you lose your prize stallion?"

She blew out a long breath. "He's my main money-maker. I could lose everything. The economy's been tough. And I'm behind on payments to the bank."

"Then maybe he took him to ruin your business. But if you don't even know him, the person who wants your business ruined has to be someone else, someone pulling the strings. This Wilkerson guy, maybe, or someone else. Who would benefit if your ranch failed?"

"No one. And even though Mr. Wilkerson and I aren't close, there's never been anything ill between us. I can't imagine him being behind this, or anyone else, really. I breed horses for people, horses that have made them a lot of money in show rings and at race-tracks. Why would anyone be mad at me for that? It doesn't make sense."

"Have you ever bred horses that didn't work out as hoped, that cost their owners money?"

"Well, sure. Breeding is both an art and a science. Even when you think you have the science part worked out, there's always the chance that the foal doesn't turn out the way you hoped. It's a gamble. But everyone knows that. No one assumes a specific horse is going to become the long-awaited champion. You hope. You plan for the possibility. But in the end, it takes dozens of mediocre foals to get one true champion." She held her hands up. "But like I said—anyone in the horse business knows that."

"What if Palmer isn't in the horse business? What if he, or someone he's working for, bought one of your horses hoping it would be the answer to their money woes, but instead the horse turned out to be a dud?"

She stiffened. "None of my horses are duds. They may not be champions, but they're not duds."

"My apologies." He had to try hard not to laugh at the indignant expression on her face. You'd have thought he'd insulted her firstborn. "I'm just saying that if someone was less…educated on the potential outcomes of a breeding program, they could have invested unwisely and lost everything. That would explain a grudge. And it could explain why Palmer said it wasn't about the horse. It was about revenge for something bigger, like someone losing their ranch."

"Well, if that's what this is about, then that's ridiculous. Hurting people over a bad investment makes no sense."

He hugged her against him. "That's because you're not the kind of person that Palmer is. You would never blame someone for something that's out of their control."

She gave him an odd look, then nodded. "You're right. I wouldn't."

Piper stopped. "Do you hear that?"

He cocked his head, concentrating. Then he heard it. It was distant, barely recognizable, but it was there. *Splashing.*

"A waterfall." He grabbed her hand in his. "You, Miss Caraway, may have just saved our lives."

She grinned. "And you, Detective Vale, owe me one. I can't wait to make you pay up."

"I don't think the *detective* will get that chance," a menacing voice called out from the darkness.

Colby shoved Piper behind his back and whipped out his knife.

Half a dozen flashlights blazed to life, forming a semicircle around them. Colby blinked, raising a hand to shield his eyes. As if at someone's signal, the beams lowered to point toward the ground.

The openly hostile looks on the faces of the four men and two women who were holding those flashlights made Palmer and his thugs look like friendly greeters at a neighborhood store.

They were each wearing a mix-and-match assortment of hats, camouflage pants and jackets, like the kind carried in an army surplus store. Thick, rubber-soled boots kept the cold and rain from freezing their feet. But this wasn't some search party out to rescue lost hikers. Every single one of them was holding a rifle, and they were all pointed at Colby.

"Drop the knife, *cop.*" The same voice they'd heard earlier nearly spit the word *cop* as if it were an obscenity. The owner of that voice, a man, stepped out from behind a tree.

Just under six feet tall, he was about Colby's height but probably carried a good twenty pounds less muscle.

"I'm Detective Colby Vale, from the Destiny Police Department," Colby announced in his most authoritative voice.

The man who'd spoken stepped a few feet closer, obviously the leader. "Destiny? Sounds like one of those stupid theme parks with a squeaky mouse mascot."

There were a few snickers behind him. Piper's hands curled against the back of Colby's shirt.

"Destiny's a small town in Blount County, about halfway between Knoxville and Maryville. What's the closest town to this place?"

The man frowned. "You don't know where you are?"

Colby shook his head. "We were abducted and dumped here. I'd appreciate it if you all could help us find our way down the mountain. Or let me borrow a phone and I'll call my men so they can come pick us up."

A low rumble of angry voices sounded behind the leader.

"Ain't no one calling no cops," the man said, and a chorus of "hell yeahs" sounded from his team. "Tell your partner to quit hiding or we'll blow a hole through the both of you."

"She's not my—" Colby stopped short when Piper stepped out beside him. He tried to shove her back. But she stepped out of reach and faced the gunmen.

"I'm Piper Caraway." She held out her hand.

He ignored her hand. "You don't look tall enough to be a cop."

She dropped her hand to her side. "My height has never stopped me from doing anything I wanted to do. And I'm not a *police officer*. I'm a horsewoman with a ranch outside Lexington. My Friesian stallion was stolen, and Detective Vale was helping me find him. He's a good man. He doesn't deserve to have a bunch of rednecks pointing guns at him."

Colby winced. He was about to grab Piper and shove her behind his back again, hoping his body would give her some protection from the bullets that were about to slam into him. But then the craziest thing happened. The leader started laughing.

Not a deep laugh, and no one else joined in. But at least no one was shooting.

The leader scrubbed the stubble on his face and shook his head. "You've got spirit, Piper. I'll give you that. You can call me Jedidiah. And all those *rednecks* behind me are my family. We don't cotton to trespassers around here. And we sure don't cotton to cops or anyone who hangs with them. Guess you could say it's bad for the neighborhood." He grinned, then raised his hand in the air and made a rolling motion.

Leaves rustled and another half-dozen camo-dressed men and women stepped from behind the trees on either side of Colby and Piper, pointing an assortment of long guns and pistols.

The leader's amusement had been short-lived. The look on his face now could only be described as menacing. He pulled a pistol from his pants pocket and pointed it directly at Piper's head, while keeping his narrow-eyed gaze on Colby.

"Drop it," he ordered.

Colby dropped the knife.

Chapter Ten

Colby rested his arms on top of his drawn-up knees, keeping watch on the door to their prison—a drafty shed the size of a small bathroom in an average household with a cold dirt floor. At least they'd been given some crackers and water last night. And before being locked up, they'd been allowed to use what amounted to a privy outside. But there was no heat in the shed, and the only concession to the temperatures were a couple of lumpy pillows and two scratchy blankets.

Piper had immediately curled up with one of those pillows and a blanket and sighed like she was in a five-star hotel. She'd been asleep about two seconds later and still hadn't woken up. Colby glanced over at her. She still had a smile on her face. He just hoped it wasn't the last time she ever smiled.

He'd allowed himself a couple hours of sleep just so he could function. But after jerking awake a little before dawn, he'd kept his vigil. Watching. Waiting. And hoping he could figure something out to save both of them from the self-proclaimed leader of this little mountain gang—Jedidiah.

The sound of feet shuffling in the dirt outside had him shaking Piper awake.

She blinked sleepily up at him. "What?"

"Get up. They're coming."

Her eyes widened, and they both scrambled to their feet.

PIPER STOOD SIDE by side with Colby in spite of his attempts to again shove her behind him. Whatever happened, she wanted to face it, not hide like a coward.

The lock clicked and the door swung open. Instead of Jedidiah, a woman stood in the opening. Or, rather, a girl. She couldn't have been more than fifteen years old, sixteen at the most. But she wasn't a "sweet" sixteen. There was nothing sweet about a teenager pointing a pistol at them.

"Out." She motioned with the gun, then backed up.

Colby looked like he wanted to charge at her, but the four armed guards outside must have made him change his mind.

"I'm Mindy," the girl said. "Dad told me y'all stink and not just because of the cop smell." She rolled her eyes as if she thought her father was a bit too dramatic with his insults. "Come on up to the house and you can both get showers and fresh clothes. Then we'll see about getting you something to eat."

Without waiting for a reply, she shoved her gun in her pocket and turned around. Piper wondered who "Dad" was. If it was Jedidiah, she wasn't too keen on going wherever this girl was leading them to.

Colby pressed a hand against the small of her back to urge her forward. The guards weren't nearly as friendly looking as the girl had been and they were all watching them closely, guns out, but at least pointing at the ground instead of at the two of them.

They followed a well-worn path through the woods, with the sun's rays breaking through the trees overhead. Just knowing that they'd survived the night and made it to a new day was enough to lift Piper's spirits.

Then she saw the *house*.

Her shoulders slumped.

Colby's hand found the small of her back again, urging her forward since Mindy was waiting for them at the door, the one that was made of vertical black bars. The whole place appeared a little bigger than the shack they'd just come from.

"Just think about getting clean," he whispered from behind her. "It looks like there's some kind of boiler outside. A hot shower sounds good, right?"

Piper drew a deep breath, then stepped through the opening under the sign that read Communal Bath.

PIPER'S FACE WAS hotter than the water from the boiler by the time she and Colby were washed, dried and dressed in the jeans and tops that Mindy gave them. Not that Colby had been anything but a gentleman. Without any dividers or even curtains between their two showers, he'd kept his eyes closed and turned away from her as much as possible as he washed himself.

She was the one who'd misbehaved.

She couldn't count the times her gaze had strayed his way, lingering far too long on the intriguing angles and planes of his body, imagining her fingers splaying across his flawless skin and exploring the rippling muscles of his abs. And his arms. Good grief, they were perfect. There was something about biceps that turned her into mush inside. And Colby's were Goldilocks perfect—not too small, not too big, just right for holding a woman or bracing himself above her as he—

"Piper?" Colby waved a hand in front of her face. "Earth to Piper?"

Her face flamed even hotter as she realized she'd been caught staring at him. Of course, he was dressed now, in a long-sleeved denim shirt and jeans that looked like they'd been made for him. So he didn't know that she was remembering how he looked naked.

His brows drew down and he pressed the back of his hand to her forehead. "Do you feel okay? You seem flushed."

She ducked away from his hand and tossed her used towel on the pile of discarded clothing where Mindy had told them to put their things after they showered.

"I'm fine. Clean, warm and wearing clean, warm clothing." She plucked at the white heavy-knit sweater she'd been given to wear over a tank and a plain but serviceable bra. "Honestly, I can't complain except for the fact that we're prisoners. Everything fits great." She wiggled her toes in the thick socks and waterproof boots she'd been given. "Even the boots fit fairly well. They're only a little too big."

"I imagine they have all kinds of supplies stockpiled so they don't have to interact with civilization too often. Makes sense they'd have something that would fit us. The fact that they're sharing their supplies is a good sign. But keep a watchful eye out. We need a good understanding of where everything is, whether there are any vehicles we could steal if it comes to that. They obviously have no love for law enforcement. And you're guilty by association."

"You think they'd actually…kill us?"

His gaze slid from hers. "Of course not. But they might want to hold us for a while to make sure we aren't a threat." He waved toward their surroundings. "It's likely they've built their compound on land that's owned and protected by the government, part of the national park system. So they wouldn't want us to share information about their location with anyone. We just need to make sure they trust us. Then they'll let us go."

"Just like that? You really think so?"

He gave her a sharp nod, but he still wasn't looking at her. She was pretty sure he was lying again to protect her from worry. And she appreciated it.

A loud rap on the wall was their signal to hurry up. They exited the building and Mindy stepped onto the path in front of them, waving for them to follow her into the woods again. Although they didn't see any guards this time, Piper assumed they were within earshot in case Mindy needed them. Maybe it was a test of sorts.

They'd probably walked about fifty yards when the path ended at another shack. This one was much larger than the others, probably four times the size of the bathhouse. The same bars covered the door and a set of windows.

"Raccoons." Mindy waved toward the windows. "Possums, too. If we don't bar all the openings, they'll get into everything. We tried chicken wire at first. Then the bears came, so we had to get the bars."

Piper gave a nervous laugh and looked around. "Have any bears poking around lately?"

Mindy gave her a droll look. "In the winter? Really?"

Colby laughed, then coughed to cover it.

Piper aimed a glare his way before following Mindy inside.

The smell of bacon had her mouth watering as soon as she stepped through the door. All her fears about bears and crazy mountain people with guns melted away when she saw the large open kitchen on one end, the rows of tables and benches that filled the rest of the space, and more importantly the food set up like a buffet on one of those tables.

"Go on," Mindy said. "Eat your fill. The rest of us already ate." She paused. "You two ain't veggie people, are you?"

Piper exchanged a confused look with Colby. "You mean vegetarians?"

Mindy nodded.

"I'm not." She arched a brow at Colby.

He snorted. "Is that a joke?"

Since Mindy looked confused, Piper clarified. "We're both meat eaters. No worries. I'm sure whatever you have will be great. Neither of us has had much to eat in the past twenty-four hours. Thank you for helping us." She waved her hands at their clothes. "Shelter, food, clothing and hot showers. We couldn't have found better rescuers."

Mindy blinked, then laughed. "Okay. Whatever." She waved toward the open kitchen, separated from the dining area by a long bar. "Don't waste your time looking for weapons in there. All the cabinets are locked up tight. So are the drawers. And unless you want to starve, I suggest you use the time I'm giving you to eat. Waste time searching this place and it just means your bellies stay empty. I'll be back in twenty." She headed out of the building.

"What a delightful little teenager," Piper grumbled.

Colby arched a brow. "Rescuers?"

"Yeah, well. Call it psychological warfare. I was trying to put the idea in her head that we're friends."

"Good luck with that. She said she'd be back in twenty. We need to be ready in ten." He grabbed them both a plate from a stack at the end of the table and started spooning scrambled eggs, potatoes and bacon onto his.

Piper scooped the same onto hers and set bottles of water in front of both of them. "To do what? Search the kitchen? She said everything was locked up."

He paused with a plastic fork full of eggs halfway to his mouth. "I didn't see any other buildings near this one, so that means the knives they use for cooking have to be in those cabinets or drawers. If I have to rip the kitchen apart to get to them, I will. Then we'll surprise Mindy." He shoveled the eggs into his mouth.

Piper frowned and picked up a piece of bacon. "Surprise her? What do you mean?" She bit off a huge bite and was pretty sure her taste buds had an orgasm. She'd never tasted anything better. Then again, it could be because she was starving.

"She's our ticket out of here." Colby kept his voice low. "I'm going to grab her gun and force her to take us to one of their vehicles."

She swallowed, the bacon no longer tasting quite so good. "How do you plan on getting her gun?"

"I'm not going to walk up and ask her for it, that's for sure. I'll do whatever I have to do."

She blinked. "But she's a teenager. A kid."

"Who's carrying a loaded Sig Sauer nine-millimeter pistol. Your point?"

"My point? My point is that I don't want her to get hurt. It's not her fault that her family's loony tunes."

He lowered his fork. "You heard her laugh when you called them our rescuers. Right? You heard that the same as I did. Why do you think she thought it was funny?"

She struggled for words, but he continued without waiting.

"Because she knows we're prisoners, not guests. Trust me. They wouldn't assign her to watch over us if they weren't one hundred percent certain she'd use that pistol if we tried to escape. Don't let her age fool you. She's just as ingrained in this culture as the rest of them. Cops are their enemies. The only reason they haven't already killed me, and you, is because they're wondering whether there's any chance someone can track us to them. As soon as they decide the answer is no, all this nice treatment stops."

She'd been trying to eat while he spoke. But her appetite died a quick death by the time he finished.

"You really believe that girl would shoot us?"

"Without blinking."

"So if we surprise her and you try to take her gun and she fights you, what then?"

"I'm a police officer. These people are criminals.

I'll do whatever I have to do to protect you and get us both out of here alive."

She waved her hands impatiently. "But what does that mean? What does that mean for Mindy?"

"It means, if I have to, I'll kill her."

ANY HOPES THAT Colby may have harbored about him and Piper remaining friends, and possibly becoming something far more than that if they survived this ordeal, evaporated the minute he told her he would kill Mindy if he had to.

The glare that Piper was giving him from across the room right now made it clear that he wasn't at the top of her favorite persons list right now. Hell, he'd probably fallen off the list altogether.

Killing Mindy wasn't something he wanted to do. In fact, it was the very last thing he *wanted* to do. Piper was right. Mindy was too young to blame for her parents' choices. But she was old enough to know that pointing a gun at someone and keeping them against their will was wrong. And if it came to a choice of saving the girl or Piper, he'd save Piper.

Even if she hated him for it.

He had to give Piper credit. Even though she was furious with him, she was still going along with his plan. She was sitting at the table to draw Mindy's attention away from Colby, who was backed against the wall beside the door, ready to wrestle the gun away from her.

As plans went, it wasn't much. But he'd thoroughly tested every window, every bar over every window, and the only way out was through that front door. There was no Plan B. He wasn't going to wait around for her to take them to Jedidiah and his band of merry criminals to decide their fate.

The lock clicked. The door swung open. Colby waited, ready to grab Mindy, but she didn't step inside.

"Where's the cop?" her voice called out from the open doorway.

Piper looked around as if in surprise. "Oh, I think he's back there, in the kitchen area." She waved toward the long countertop that separated the open kitchen from the dining tables. "I'm afraid we made a bit of a mess and he's cleaning it up."

"A mess?"

Piper's face turned red, probably because she was nervous about their plan. She shrugged and gave a nervous laugh. "We dropped some plates back there. You should just wait outside. No sense in risking getting cut. Isn't that right, Colby?" She looked over her shoulder toward the kitchen as if waiting for his reply.

Mindy took a tentative step into the room, her pistol out in front of her.

Colby didn't wait for a second step. He lunged toward her, wrenching the gun out of her hand and yanking her back from the doorway. Piper jumped up and closed the door as he clasped a hand over Mindy's mouth to keep her from screaming. The girl picked her feet up from beneath her, an old trick he'd been expecting. He simply clasped her hard against his chest and slid to the floor with her still in his arms.

It took a couple of minutes to wear her out and get her to stop struggling. Her chest was heaving from exertion and her face was slick with sweat.

Colby glanced up at Piper standing a few feet away,

her brow crinkled with worry. But that worry wasn't directed at him. She was worried about the little miscreant in his arms.

"She's fine," he bit out. "I'm fine, too. Thanks for asking."

Piper rolled her eyes. "What do we do now?"

"Take the gun."

She surprised him by taking it without hesitation. She pointed it at the floor, her finger on the frame instead of the trigger.

"Don't look so surprised," she told him. "I may not be a police officer, but I know my way around guns. My daddy taught me how to shoot, too."

"And I'm very appreciative that he did."

Keeping his hand cupped over the girl's mouth so she couldn't scream or bite him, he pulled the dish towels out of his jacket pocket that he'd grabbed from the kitchen while formulating his plan. She couldn't see that he had the dishcloths, so she didn't know what he was going to do. He held one cloth in his free hand, rolled into a ball. Then, he yanked his other hand off her mouth. She immediately opened her mouth to scream. Before she could make a sound, he stuffed the balled-up cloth inside and cupped his hand on top again.

Twisting with her in his arms, he rolled her onto her belly with her hands trapped underneath her and sat on her, effectively trapping her.

But that didn't stop her from slamming her heels into his back.

Piper surprised him yet again by hopping onto

Mindy's legs and holding them down. He glanced over his shoulder at her.

"Thanks."

"I'm helping you wrestle a child. I'm going to hell for this and I blame you. Do *not* thank me."

He chuckled, then secured the gag with two more dish towels that he'd tied together earlier. Then he sat back and waited. Sure enough, the scrappy teen tried to scream. But it came out muffled and could barely be heard. The balled-up dish towel being held in place by more dish towels might have been crude, but it was working.

He gave her a quick frisk but didn't find anything else on her, which surprised him. A kid her age usually had a cell phone attached to their hip. He leaned down again, careful to keep his head out of head-butting range.

"Mindy, we don't want to hurt you. If you help us get out of here, we'll let you go. No harm done."

She tried to head-butt him, just as he'd anticipated. All she managed to do was slam her jaw against the floor. Her cry of pain was low but discernible, even through the gag.

"What did you do to her?" Piper demanded.

"Nothing. She did it to herself."

"Did what?"

"Hit her chin on the floor."

Piper's sharp intake of breath was his only warning before she jumped up and hurried over to Mindy's head. The girl wasted no time in slamming her heels into his back again.

Thump. Thump. Thump.

He rolled his eyes while Piper bent down on her knees and gently moved the hair out of Mindy's face.

"Are you okay, sweetie? Did you bite your tongue? Do you need—"

Mindy twisted violently and snaked a hand out from under her, grabbing Piper's wrist—the one holding the pistol.

Colby swore and grabbed Mindy's forearm. He pressed down, hard, on her radial nerve. Her fingers flew open and she cried out in pain against the gag.

He grabbed the gun. But instead of thanking him for staving off a disaster, Piper glared at him.

"You said you weren't going to hurt her," she accused.

"I said I would *try* not to hurt her. She gave me no choice. Maybe I should just shoot her and wait for someone more docile to run in to check on her and grab them instead."

Mindy immediately grew still. The only sign that she was still alive was her ragged breathing against the gag.

Colby took advantage of her sudden acquiescence and hopped off her. He checked the pistol, shoved it into the pocket of his jacket, then jerked her upright. Another pile of tied-together dishcloths lay on the floor behind the door. He grabbed them and tied her hands behind her back, then whirled her around to face him.

"You're going to cooperate?"

She nodded enthusiastically.

"Why?"

She gave him an are-you-an-idiot look and pointed to her gag.

He grinned. "Right. Can't answer my question." He looked over his shoulder. "Piper? Ready?"

"As I'll ever be. I can't believe we're doing this."

"Would you rather wait for Jedidiah to come back with his fellow fruitcakes and pass judgment?"

"When you put it that way…"

He held the gun out to her again. "Check the loading."

She popped the magazine out. "It's full." She slammed it back in and held the gun down by her side.

"You know there's no safety on a Sig, right? Just point and shoot."

Mindy jerked against him.

"Cool it," he warned. "As long as you cooperate and your friends like you enough to want to keep you alive, everyone comes out of this okay."

Her brow wrinkled with worry.

He sighed. "Teenager. I forgot. Don't worry. I'm sure your family wants to keep you alive even if you're rebellious and a complete pain in the butt. Okay?"

Her brow smoothed out and she nodded.

Colby wasn't fooled. He didn't expect her to cooperate. But it didn't really matter. One of the crazies outside was her father. That was the connection Colby was counting on to keep them safe.

He reached into his boot and pulled out the knife he'd tucked inside just moments before Mindy had arrived.

Her eyes widened when she saw it.

"I might have destroyed a couple of the drawers in your kitchen," he admitted.

She tried to twist away from him. He yanked her

back and pressed the dull back edge of the knife against her skin. She didn't know it wasn't the sharp edge and grew still as soon as she felt the cold steel.

"I don't want to hurt you, Mindy. I really don't. But I can skewer you in far less time than it would take any of your buddies out there to reach me."

She didn't move, barely even breathed.

Guilt slashed through him but he ruthlessly pushed it back. He had to focus on protecting Piper or he'd get her killed. He couldn't allow himself to dwell on the psychological damage he could be inflicting on this teenager.

His shoulders slumped. Who was he kidding? He didn't want to hurt this girl in any way. He gritted his teeth and sent a pleading look at Piper.

Her expression softened with understanding. "It's okay, Colby. You're doing what you have to do. She'll be all right."

He swallowed hard, then gave her a grateful nod. This was killing him, and she knew it. And she didn't hate him. For now, that was enough.

Would the gunmen outside realize the dull edge of the knife was pressed against Mindy's throat? Would they risk her life, hoping they could shoot him before he could flip the knife's edge? He honestly didn't know. All he was sure of was that he couldn't hold a young teenager in front of him as his hostage with the cutting edge of a knife against her carotid and risk a stumble or bump, ending her life. It was the fatal flaw in his plan. But there was nothing he could do about it.

"You're a good man," Piper told him, obviously understanding his dilemma.

"I'm an idiot. You sure you want to go through with this?"

"I wasn't sure before. Now I am. Let's do this."

She took the lead, per their plan, and stepped outside.

Chapter Eleven

Colby followed Piper outside the building, one arm around Mindy's waist, the other holding the knife against her throat. The three of them stopped just a few feet outside the door, in a tight group as if they were one person, with Piper's gun pointing straight out in front of her. Colby had originally wanted it pointed at Mindy, but she'd refused. He couldn't be mad at her over it. After all, he was just as guilty, not wanting to hold the sharp knife edge against the kid's throat.

God help them both.

Colby counted twenty rifles aimed at them before he stopped counting. Jedidiah, as before, kept his pistol holstered at his waist and stood slightly in front of the others. The question of Mindy's father's identity was answered with one look at Jedidiah's face. It was ghostly white.

His Adam's apple bobbed several times before he spoke. "Let my daughter go, *cop*."

"Sure. Just as soon as you call my SWAT team in Destiny. Put them on speaker so I can hear them and talk to them."

"We don't have any phones here. No electronics. It's not our way of life."

"I don't believe you."

"Did you see any electric outlets or light switches in the buildings you've been in? We use wood-burning stoves to heat water. That boiler in the bathhouse runs on an oil and gas mixture we barter for when we go into town. The stove in the kitchen runs on gas. We don't have any phones."

Colby still wasn't sure if he believed him. A phone would have made everything so much easier.

Something moved off to his left.

"Piper, my nine o'clock. Do you see them?"

She swung her pistol in that direction. "Yep. You want me to shoot him?"

The person who'd started sneaking up on them hurried backward to get in line with the others.

"Only if they try it again."

"No problem. I'll start making a list." She scanned her pistol on the crowd like a pro. "Anyone else want to be on my shoot-first list?"

No one moved.

"Spoilsports," she grumbled.

Colby coughed. "How far away is the town?"

"What town?" Jedidiah asked.

"The one where you get the fuel oil for your boiler."

"Oh, yeah, pretty far away. A couple of days' hike."

"You don't hike through the mountains for days to bring back fuel oil and fresh food like you have in your kitchen. You've got cars or trucks. Where are they?"

"Nope, no cars. Like I said, no tech—"

"Stop lying, Jedidiah. Before I gagged your girl

here, I interrogated her." If anything, Jedidiah looked even more pale than he had earlier. Colby wondered if his hatred of the police was because of his own personal experiences. Judging by how the word *interrogated* affected him, probably so.

"She told me about the cars. But just in case she lied, I want you to go with us. You can lead the way. Take one wrong step, and she dies. Tell everyone else to back off. If I hear a footstep or even the snap of a twig while we're heading to the cars, I'll carve my anger out on your kid's flesh. You got that? No one follows us."

Jedidiah's gaze flicked to Piper's right side for just a second.

Bam!

A man fell down onto the dirt, clutching his arm, moaning in agony.

Piper cursed. "Why did you make me do that? Colby told all of you not to move! Did you think he was bluffing?"

Colby was so proud of her that he wanted to hug her. Instead, he kept his face carefully blank, as if Piper hadn't just surprised the heck out of him.

"One down. Who's next, Jedidiah? Mindy?" Colby took a risk and flipped his knife over, sharp edge poised half an inch from the girl's throat.

"No, no, stop!" Jedidiah raised his hands and motioned to his people. "Everybody back. I mean it. Latham, give me the keys to the Charger. The rest of you, go back to the meeting lodge and wait for me there. No one, under any circumstances, follows us."

There was some grumbling from the circle of men and women.

"Do it!" Jedidiah yelled.

The guns lowered toward the ground and the group dispersed, heading down a path behind Jedidiah, apparently toward the meeting lodge.

Another man ran up to him and tossed him some keys.

Jedidiah shoved them in his pocket and waved at the injured man. "Help him to the lodge. Get Vicky to see to his wound."

Colby waited while the injured man and Latham slowly made their way after the others. He was shocked that his bluff was working so well so far. The car thing was a total guess. Maybe he really should have interrogated Mindy. No telling what she might have told him.

"All right, Jedidiah. Take us to the car. Remember, one wrong turn and I carve the cost of my annoyance out of Mindy's flesh."

If hatred was a living animal, it would have leaped from Jedidiah's eyes and shredded Colby into a thousand pieces right then and there. Instead, Jedidiah gave him a sharp nod and whirled around, leading the way down a path Colby hadn't even noticed before, tucked up beside the kitchen building.

Piper gave him a questioning glance. He nodded and she started after their reluctant leader, with Colby and Mindy bringing up the rear.

As soon as they had some tree cover, Colby flipped the dull side of the knife toward Mindy's throat and leaned down close to her ear.

"Don't be afraid, Mindy. I promise I won't hurt you, no matter what your father does or doesn't do. I'm completely bluffing. I'm not going to make you pay the price for what he's done. Okay?"

A mixture of relief and distrust stared back at him. He didn't know if she believed him or not, but he'd at least had to try. The threats he'd made to her father had to have terrified her. And he couldn't stand the guilt. He didn't want her scared. He just needed her to help them get away.

He glanced behind them to make sure no one was following, then hurried to catch up with the others.

The trail ended at a parking lot of sorts beside a river. Six cars and two pickup trucks sat at various angles in between trees with camouflage netting rigged overhead so no planes or helicopters would see them.

"Paranoid much, Jedidiah?" Colby motioned toward the netting.

"It's not paranoia if it's true, cop." He gestured toward his daughter.

"You started this. I'm finishing it." Remembering that the man had directed his lackey to give him the keys to a Charger, he motioned toward the only Charger there. "Start it up."

His jaw tight, he did as Colby asked, sliding behind the wheel and turning over the engine.

"Get out."

Jedidiah hopped out and backed away from the car.

That was too easy. Something was wrong. Colby leaned into the car and checked the back seat, then the front again. It was a newer model, the kind that didn't require a key in the ignition, just a push of a button to start it. And the key was nowhere to be seen. Which meant once he got the car down the road, it would start beeping constantly as a warning. And he'd never be able to get it started again if he shut it off or even put it into Park.

He turned around. "Good try. Toss me the key."

Jedidiah motioned toward his daughter. "Let her go and you can have the key with my blessing."

"Piper?"

She raised a brow in question.

"If Mindy tries to run, shoot her."

Piper's eyes widened, then her expression smoothed out. He sensed it was taking considerable effort to pretend his outrageous comment didn't bother her. But it didn't show in her expression.

"Of course." She kept the gun trained on the ground, but faced Mindy like a hawk eyeing a field mouse.

Wow, she was good at this. He wasn't so sure that was a good thing anymore.

"If Jedidiah does anything threatening, shoot him, too."

"That goes without saying," she said drolly.

Colby had a feeling she wouldn't mind executing that order one bit. From the dark look on the other man's face, he realized it, as well.

"Let's try this again. I'm the one calling the shots now. Toss me the key."

The key sailed through the air like a missile. But Colby still managed to catch it. He'd have laughed at the juvenile antics if he wasn't worried about getting Piper out of there safely. There was no telling how long the rest of the crew would obey Jedidiah's order to stay put.

He ducked his head inside the car again and was relieved to see that the tank was full. At least he didn't have to worry about running out of gas. He motioned toward Piper and she backed toward the car. A few seconds later, she yanked the passenger door open and hopped inside, gun still pointed at their captor.

Mindy ran to her father. Colby hopped into the driver's seat and slammed the door, then floored the gas, fishtailing the car on the dirt and leaves before the tires caught. The powerful engine shot the car forward like a slingshot, propelling them down what amounted to a homemade road of hard-packed dirt with some gravel here and there in the low spots.

Piper reached across him, her face inches from his as he steered them over the bumps and around the curves.

"Seat belt," she explained, grabbing it and pulling it across his hips, then snapping it closed.

"Thanks."

"Thank *you*," she said as she cranked up the heater. After clicking her own seat belt, she let out a ragged breath. "I can't believe we're finally getting off this mountain." She took another deep breath, then another. "I didn't think we were going to make it. I thought we were going to die up there. First Palmer, then the rain and freezing and starving, and then… And then—" She covered her face with her hands and started crying.

Colby silently called Palmer and Jedidiah every foul word he could think of. As soon as he got Piper to safety, he was going to pull together every resource the Destiny Police Department had and put them both in prison for a very long time.

"It'll be okay," he told her, hating that he couldn't

risk pulling over to hold her in case Jedidiah or his groupies came after them. And the road, which was barely wide enough for the car to pass, required both hands on the steering wheel to keep from ramming the car into a tree. "Just think about getting home to your family. I mean friends. By this time tomorrow you'll be at your ranch, safe and sound."

She dropped her hands and gave him a stricken look. "Without Gladiator. I've been so worried about you and me that I completely forgot about Gladiator. Again."

"He's too remarkable a horse to go unnoticed. Heck, the guys back in Destiny have probably already found him and are holding him for you while they follow leads to hunt down Palmer."

She rubbed her eyes. "You think so?"

"I do. It's all going to work out. You're a strong woman, Piper Caraway. No one else I know could have handled everything we've been through as well as you. You rock."

She sat up a little straighter and offered him a quick smile. "You're not so bad yourself, Colby Vale. If I was going to lose my marbles and expose myself and practically attack a man I barely knew in order to stay warm, well, I can't imagine someone else I'd rather do it with."

He laughed. "Good to know." He steered around another tree, then slowed for a curve coming up. "Once you've got Gladiator back, maybe you could make a pit stop at my dad's before heading back home. He's retired now, but he still has a good dozen horses. He'd go nuts over yours."

"Will you go there with me?"

"Of course."

"Then it's a date." She coughed. "I mean, you know, an, um, appointment, or—"

"A date." He glanced over at her. "It's a date."

Her entire face lit up. "Well, okay, then."

He grinned.

Her eyes flew open wide. "Colby, look out!"

He jerked around to see an enormous pickup on a jacked-up suspension barrel out of the trees onto the road in front of them.

"Hang on!" He slammed the brakes and twisted the wheel hard right. The Charger slid sideways.

Piper screamed.

The driver's side slammed against one of the pickup's monster-size tires.

The inside of the car exploded in a hail of white dust as the airbags deployed. Colby and Piper jerked hard against their seat belts. For a moment, neither of them moved. Everything was eerily silent. The Charger's engine had stopped, probably because Jedidiah was standing about thirty feet from the car, pressing a button on something that was some kind of kill switch. Or maybe it was just how these newer cars were programmed to respond in a crash. Colby didn't have any experience with these push-button models. All he knew was that someone was pounding a sledgehammer against the inside of his skull again. And he and Piper were in serious trouble.

He forced his eyes to stay open even though all he wanted to do was curl up in the fetal position and tell God to take his pain-racked body home. He looked at Piper, and relief curled through his body like a soothing balm when he didn't see any blood. She was awake, alert and staring at him, or past him, with a mixture of worry and fear.

"Me or them?" He waved an aching hand toward the windshield. Standing on the road, heading toward the car, were the same dozen devils who'd surrounded them last night. And once again they were aiming their rifles straight at him.

"You," she exclaimed. "Your head cracked the side window. You're bleeding again." She unclipped her seat belt and tossed it off her, then climbed over the center console, punching down the airbags to get to him.

"Me?" He pressed a hand against his head. It came away slippery with fresh blood. "Great. We don't have time for this."

She shoved his hand away and put her own on top of the wound.

He hissed at the sizzle of pain that shot through his scalp.

"Quit being such a cream puff," she ordered. "I have to stop the bleeding."

He let out a bark of laughter, then winced at the pain that caused. "Cream puff? Really?"

"Just hold still." She pressed the her hand harder against the wound, sending a fresh wave of pain burning across his nerve endings.

He cursed beneath his breath.

"And stop whining," she added.

He grinned. He couldn't help it. This woman was perfect.

The passenger door jerked open behind her, and Jedidiah leaned into the opening. "Get out."

Piper whipped out the pistol that Colby had completely forgotten about and aimed it at Jedidiah's head.

"Give me an excuse to pull the trigger, you self-righteous, hypocritical, good-for-nothing idiot."

Jedidiah blinked, then stepped back, holding his hands in the air. "All right. I might deserve some of that, but I'm not sure what the hypocritical part is about."

"Really?" She waved the gun to encompass the car, while keeping her other hand on Colby's head. "No technology? No electricity? I'm guessing the bit about not having a phone is a lie, too."

He crossed his arms. "There are twelve rifles pointed at you. And your cop boyfriend is bleeding like the pig he is. How long do you think either of you will last if we start shooting?"

"Put the gun down," Colby whispered.

Her jaw tightened. "No. I won't. I'm done, Colby. I can't go back there. I just can't."

He put his hand on her cheek.

She bit her lip but kept her gun pointed at Jedidiah without looking at Colby.

"Sweetheart." He kept his voice low. "After everything we've been through, this is nothing. A piece of cake. You can do it. You're strong."

She shook her head. "No," she whispered miserably, the gun shaking in her hand. And unlike before, her finger wasn't on the frame.

It was on the trigger.

Jedidiah was turning white as he watched the pistol shake in her trembling hands.

Colby hated himself for what he was about to do.

But he didn't have a choice. If he let Piper pull that trigger, they were both dead. Twelve guns would open fire, and it would all be over. Their only chance was to give up, for now. And if she couldn't be strong at this moment, then he'd just have to be strong enough for both of them. Hopefully she'd forgive him later. But if she didn't, he was okay with that, too. As long as she *survived.*

He jammed his thumb in front of the trigger and wrenched the gun away from her.

She blinked in shock.

"Forgive me," he whispered.

Jedidiah grabbed the gun from him and yanked Piper backward out of the car.

"No!" she screamed, fighting like a rabid bobcat.

Colby winced at the sound of her screams but he could no longer see what was happening to her. He was being pulled out of the car, too, none too gently. Two men dragged him across the road to the edge of the curve, which ended up being the top of a cliff. Below, a river roiling with rapids splashed and thundered through the mountain. He couldn't believe he hadn't heard it inside the car. The noise was deafening.

Then again, maybe that was the sound of the hammer pounding inside his skull again. He was woozy. Sharp pain buzzed down his shoulders. His hands were going numb. He didn't think that was a good sign.

After patting him down for weapons, the men left him sitting there. Apparently, they didn't think he was a threat anymore. They joined the others with their leader on the far side of the road.

Colby pressed a hand to his head, realizing he

needed to stop the bleeding or he'd pass out and couldn't help Piper. But where was she?

He looked around, trying to locate the little pixie who was fast becoming more important to him than he'd ever thought anyone outside his immediate family could ever be. Without taking the time to analyze the reasons, he whipped his head around, ignoring the pounding.

"Piper? Piper, where are you?"

"Here. I'm over here."

He whipped back to his left, a ragged breath escaping him when he saw Mindy leading her toward him. She looked unharmed but mad as hell. Good. If she was mad, it would help her stand up to Jedidiah and fight to survive.

She plopped down beside him. "I'm going to make you pay for that."

"I know."

She sighed and scooted closer, her thigh pressing against his as they both watched the meeting happening on the other side of the road. Mindy stood not too far from them, holding a pistol.

"Just like old times," Piper said, giving Mindy a hard look before looking back at the others. "They're probably drawing straws to see who gets to kill us."

"Well, you did wreck Pa's favorite car," Mindy said.

Piper gave her an incredulous look.

Mindy rolled her eyes and kicked her shoe at the rocks at the edge.

"Let me check that gash." Piper peeled his hand away. "Not nearly as bad as I thought it was. Probably doesn't even need stitches. Head wounds always bleed so much, it's hard to tell how bad they are. The bleeding's almost stopped."

"Thanks."

She rested her head on his shoulder. "We're in this together. I can't afford to be mad at you right now."

"But when we get off the mountain?"

"*If* we get off the mountain—"

"*When.*"

"—then I'll figure out some way for you to make all of this up to me."

"Deal."

She gave him a weary smile. "All I ask is that before I die, someone please explain to me why Todd Palmer chose me as his victim, then dragged you into it."

"Todd Palmer?" Mindy called out. "You know Palmer?"

Colby and Piper both turned to look at her.

"*You* know him?" Colby asked.

"Not exactly," she hedged. "I may have heard of him, though."

"How?" they both said.

She shrugged, obviously not keen on revealing anything else about herself or her family. "He did something to you guys?"

"If you call stealing my horse, forging a bill of sale, kidnapping Colby and me, ordering his men to kill us, then leaving us stranded in these mountains without supplies or even shoes for our feet, doing something, um, yeah. He did something to us. And if we ever get away from your psycho family, we'll both hunt him down and send him to prison, unless I can figure out a way to make an accident happen to him first."

Mindy's eyes widened like small moons.

Colby coughed to keep from grinning at her empty threat. By now he'd learned enough about her to realize she could be tough when she needed to be. But she was also honorable and kind. He couldn't imagine her really doing anything to hurt Palmer no matter how much she wanted to, unless it was to save herself or someone else. But maybe she really believed what she was saying, because she aimed a glare his way.

He grinned but didn't dare laugh.

Unamused, she pursed her lips and walked to his far side. She sat down about ten feet from him and Mindy.

"Kind of ornery, isn't she?" Mindy asked.

"After what she's been through, I think she's earned the right. Don't you?"

The girl shrugged, then cupped her hands together. "Hey, Pa," she yelled. "These two are on the run from that Palmer fellow. He stole their horse."

Jedidiah turned around, and his group fell silent as all eyes focused on Colby and Piper.

"Where is he?" Jedidiah demanded.

Colby shook his head. "I have no idea. Probably at some auction house somewhere, selling Piper's prize Friesian stallion. He didn't exactly give us a forwarding address when he took off, leaving us in the woods with two gunmen with orders to kill us."

"He's your enemy?"

"He's a suspect and I aim to arrest him and get to the bottom of his crimes."

"I hope you shoot him," Mindy said beneath her breath.

Colby looked her way, then jumped to his feet.

"Mindy, come away from the edge. The rocks are loose. You could—"

The ground began crumbling beneath her. She cried out, her arms cartwheeling as she desperately tried to keep her balance.

Colby dived toward her but fell short, his fingers just brushing the hem of her jeans. The ledge gave way, sending her crashing into the roiling water below.

"Help!" she screamed. "Can't swim!" Her pale, terrified face disappeared beneath the surface.

"Mindy!" Jedidiah yelled.

"Colby, don't!" Piper begged. "It's too dangerous!"

Colby pushed off the ledge and dived into the river below.

Chapter Twelve

Piper dropped to her knees at the edge of the crumbling cliff and looked down into the treacherous water below, desperately searching for Colby. He'd disappeared beneath the surface and hadn't come back up.

Jedidiah plopped down beside her. "Where is she? Where's…" His voice broke and his Adam's apple bobbed in his throat. "Where's Mindy?"

Piper's face flooded with heat. How terrible that she hadn't given a single thought to the young girl who was struggling for her life down there, too. All she could think about was Colby.

The color had blanched from Jedidiah's face, leaving it mottled and pale. His friends stood in a half circle behind him, looking just as frightened as he did as they scanned the river beneath the cliff. No matter how messed up these people were or what crazy views they held, in the end they were just as human as everyone else. And someone they loved—who couldn't swim— had just gone into nearly freezing water with a swift current and tumbling rapids.

"I haven't seen her or Colby." She jumped to her feet and shrugged off her coat.

"What are you doing?" Jedidiah demanded, pushing himself to standing.

"Going in after them." She moved to the edge, drew in a deep breath—

"No." He grabbed her arm in a viselike grip. "It's too dangerous. I heard you yelling that at your cop boyfriend. And you were right." He drew a ragged breath. "No one could survive down there."

She shoved at his hand. "Well, someone has to at least try to help them." She aimed a glare at the other men. "If no one has the guts to go in after them, I will. Now, let me go while there's still a chance."

He shook his head again, his hand tightening painfully on her biceps. "It would be suicide. They're gone." He let out a ragged breath. "Latham, tie her up if you have to. No one else goes into that river."

Piper cursed and fought, fingers like talons striking out at Latham, her legs flailing in the air as he jerked her up and away from the edge. He let out a few choice swear words when she slammed her shoe down hard against his thigh. But he simply clamped an arm around hers and trapped her between his legs in a show of strength surprising for his size, rendering her defenseless.

"Let me go!" she cried out. "They're going to die if no one helps them. What are you? Cowards? Mindy's just a kid. Colby's an innocent man risking his own life for your daughter and friend." She tossed her head, skewering each of them with her glare. When no one moved to do anything, she cursed again. "What's *wrong* with you people? One of your own is drowning and you're standing around doing nothing!"

"I don't know how to swim," Jedidiah admitted, hanging his head in shame. "None of us do. And I can't let you kill yourself because of our failures. It wouldn't be right."

She blinked at him in shock. "*Now* you're getting a conscience?"

He gritted his teeth and looked away. "Mindy's gone. There's nothing we can—"

"Daddy!"

He whirled around.

Mindy, ghostly pale and dripping wet, ran out of the trees on the other side of the road. Colby was right behind her, just as wet and pale.

"Mindy, my God. Mindy." Jedidiah ran to her and folded her in his arms. Great rasping sobs shook his shoulders as everyone surrounded them, just as choked with emotion.

Piper ran to Colby, stopping right in front of him. She lifted shaking hands and pushed his wet hair back from his face.

"Are you okay?" The words had to be forced through her thick throat.

He nodded. "I reached her right away but the current kept us from surfacing. I had to pull her across the bottom of the river until we escaped the current. Thankfully she knew enough to at least hold her breath most of that time. I had to pump a little water out of her. But overall, I think she'll be okay. She just needs to get warmed up."

"Oh, Colby. Here I am concerned about you, asking about you, and all you do is give me a report about the daughter of a madman. A girl who would probably shoot us both if ordered to by her father or one of his followers." She cupped his face between her hands. "Why did you risk your life like that?"

He frowned, as if the question made no sense. "Because I was the closest one. There was no time to wait for someone else to do it."

"You're an amazing man, Colby Vale." She stood on tiptoe and pulled him down so that she could press a kiss against his lips. They were so cold that tears filled her eyes. "You're freezing. We need to get you warm and dry before you die of hypothermia."

"Yes. We do." The voice sounded behind her.

She turned to see Jedidiah approaching both of them with their coats and a blanket in his hands. Mindy was being led to one of the cars by Latham, another blanket thrown around her shoulders. But instead of the rest of them surrounding Colby and Piper with their guns, they were heading to the other vehicles.

He held out the blanket to Colby. "Here, dry off, then put your coat back on before you get sick."

Colby gave him a suspicious look and ignored the blanket, instead taking the coat meant for Piper and putting it around her shoulders. Then he took the blanket.

"What's your game this time?" Colby sloughed the water off him and rubbed the blanket against his hair. "Let me guess. You want me dry so I don't get the inside of one of the cars wet when you drive us back to your little prison."

Piper grabbed the other coat. Colby tossed the wet blanket at Jedidiah and let Piper help him into the coat.

"I deserve your mistrust. I know," Jedidiah said. "But you have to understand, we never would have hurt either of you. We took care of you—gave you shelter, fed you, let you have a hot shower, clothed you."

"You *sheltered* us in a freezing shed and kept us under armed guard. We were your prisoners."

"Only to protect you, and to protect us, too. We weren't sure who you were, whether you meant us harm. And we couldn't just let you wander back down the mountain on your own. Something could have happened to you. We were still trying to figure out what to do."

"We told you who we were, that I was a police officer."

"You didn't have any identification on you. We couldn't just take your word."

"You knew I was a cop. That's why you spit the word *cop* at me as if it was an insult."

Piper glanced back and forth between them, noting the anger and frustration on Colby's face, probably because they'd been so close to getting away. And now they were back to square one. He was once again cold and wet and contemplating being locked up. She was just as angry as he was. But when she turned to blister Jedidiah with her own rage, her anger died underneath a wall of confusion. Jedidiah didn't look like a dangerous criminal. He looked like a broken man, his shoulders slumping beneath guilt and pain. And he didn't even have a gun as far as she could see.

"We were protecting our home—"

"That doesn't give you the right to kidnap us," Colby told him.

"I know, I know. I'm sorry."

Colby frowned and exchanged a surprised look with Piper.

"You're sorry?" Colby asked.

He nodded. "We would have let you go eventually. But I'll let you go now with my blessing, and a car." He dug some keys from his pocket and held them out to Colby. "Mindy's Mustang is over there, just past the Charger. You can have it."

Colby didn't move, just watched Jedidiah with open suspicion as if he was a rattler ready to strike.

"Let's get out of here, Colby." Piper grabbed the keys, then tried to pull him toward the Mustang. The truck had been moved and the others were in their vehicles, leaving the dented Charger sitting in the road where they'd left it. But true to Jedidiah's word, a dark blue Mustang, several years old but looking in good condition, sat about fifty yards away and appeared to be empty. "Come on. Let's go."

"You're just letting us go?" Colby stood ramrod straight, still facing Jedidiah in spite of Piper's attempts at tugging him toward the car. "You plan on following us and ramming us again when we're driving near a cliff?"

Jedidiah held his hands up as if in surrender. "As you probably guessed already, we don't own the land we're living on. We didn't figure we were hurting anyone, but then you came along and I felt I had to protect what was ours. Or what we'd taken." He cleared his throat. "I was wrong. We were wrong. You saved my little girl. I owe you more than I could ever repay."

"Then give me a phone."

He shook his head. "I wasn't lying about not having any phones. We have cars, trucks, because they're necessary up this far when we need supplies. Or if we have to leave in a hurry. But that's not how we live day to day. We live off the land. No electronics."

"Just really expensive guns," Colby sneered.

Jedidiah's face reddened. "For hunting deer. To feed our families."

Piper didn't know whether to believe the man or not. But she didn't want to stand here arguing when they could be making a run for it.

"How do we get out of the mountains? Where's the nearest home or business with a phone?"

"There's a GPS map in the car."

"No electronics, huh?" Colby asked, sarcasm dripping from every word.

Jedidiah frowned, his growing anger overtaking his guilt. "I couldn't risk Mindy getting lost when she had to drive into town. Just scroll through recent trips on the GPS screen. There's a bait and tackle shop at the end of this road. They'll have a phone and anything else you might need." He raked a hand through his hair. "I've given you coats and a car with a full gas tank. That's the best I can do. Either take the car or don't. But if you get lost or freeze to death in these mountains, then that's on you. I appreciate you saving my little girl. And this is me repaying you."

With that, he motioned to his men, and the cars started pulling onto the road, heading away from them.

Colby pulled Piper closer to him, as if ready to make a dash for it. But Jedidiah paid him no mind as he headed toward his daughter, who was standing by a pickup. Latham, the only other man whose name they knew, had cut away the airbag hanging over the steering wheel in the Charger and slid in behind the wheel. Soon he was heading after the others, leaving only the Mustang and Jedidiah's pickup.

"If he wanted to kill us, he could have shot us already." Piper tugged Colby's sleeve. "Come on. Let's go before he changes his mind."

He finally relented and they hurried to the Mustang.

"I'll drive," Piper said. "You need to sit in front of the heater and dry out before you catch pneumonia."

She expected him to argue. After all, he was protective with a capital *P* and probably thought it was his duty to drive them off of the mountain. But his movements were sluggish and his face was still alarmingly pale. His wet clothes certainly weren't helping.

"I don't suppose you'd consider stripping and laying your clothes in the back window to dry?"

He rolled his eyes. "Stop worrying about me. And no way am I going to risk being caught butt naked if something happens again." He got in on the passenger side.

"Pity," she said, thinking she would have enjoyed having naked Colby sit next to her.

Then again, maybe all that golden skin and rippling muscles would have been too distracting. She slid behind the wheel and turned the key, relieved to hear it roar to life. She didn't trust Jedidiah any more than Colby and had half expected the offer of a car to be a cruel trick. She cranked up the heater and aimed the vents toward Colby while keeping an eye on the truck on the far side of the road with Jedidiah and Mindy inside.

Mindy huddled in her blanket. She waved and Piper waved back. Colby didn't seem to notice. His fingers appeared to be cramping from the cold as he struggled with his seat belt.

"Why don't you ever ask for help?" She chastised him and grabbed the seat belt, when what she really wanted to do was cry. He was one of the most honorable men she'd ever met. It was so unfair that he'd suffered so much. She clicked the belt closed.

A knock sounded on the driver's widow, startling her.

Colby jumped, too, unclicking his seat belt and leaning over her protectively in about two seconds flat. Piper couldn't help but smile even though his shoulder was painfully pressing hers back into the seat.

"What do you want?" he demanded of Jedidiah, who stood on the other side of the glass.

"Mindy said Todd Palmer stole your horse."

Colby frowned, then clicked a button and rolled down the window. "What of it?"

"Let's just say that Palmer has made the rounds. He doesn't exactly have any friends on this mountain. Any idea where he went?"

"None."

"What was he driving? What did the horse look like?"

Colby didn't seem eager to tell him, so Piper pressed his shoulder, getting him to ease back a few inches so she could talk to Jedidiah.

"He stole my rig—a blue F-350 pickup truck with a

custom matching trailer. *Caraway Ranch* is written on the side. There were two horses inside. A bay gelding and a black Friesian stallion named Gladiator. Why are you asking?"

He straightened and offered them a bland smile. "You two be careful. The road can be sketchy this time of year." With that, he hurried back to his truck.

Piper and Colby watched as he pulled down the road, then disappeared around the curve.

Colby punched the button, rolling the window back up. "Let's get out of here before he comes back with a rifle."

"Gladly." She helped him fasten the seat belt again, then punched the gas and headed down the road.

True to Jedidiah's word, the GPS maps led them down the dirt road and off of the mountain to a gravel road with a bait store off to one side. But when she would have pulled in, Colby grabbed the steering wheel.

"Don't stop. Keep going down this road until we reach a highway."

"You think the store is a trap?"

"It doesn't make sense that it would be, since he let us go. But I'm not willing to take any chances."

"Then we'll keep going." It about killed her to pass the store and continue down the gravel road without turning in. There were two cars parked out front, which meant other people—civilization, help. But she trusted Colby's instincts. After all, he was a police officer. He dealt with the worst types of people out there and knew far better than her what kinds of twisted games they might play.

Nearly an hour later they reached a sign for a highway, a two-lane, extremely rural highway, but it was paved and well maintained. She didn't think she'd ever seen a more beautiful road. Ten minutes after that, they were inside a truck stop manager's office.

Soon, Colby was on the phone with the local police, giving them a brief explanation of what had happened and asking that they send a cruiser to pick him and Piper up.

As it turned out, they were in Johnson County, Tennessee—not far from Mountain City, a town of about eighteen thousand residents. It sat in the northeast corner of the state, in the Blue Ridge Mountains, a three-hour drive from Destiny if you took the major highways instead of the winding back roads Palmer had taken to dump them in the wilderness. And a whopping five-hour drive to her home in Lexington. No wonder neither she nor Colby had recognized the scenery. Neither of them had ever been here before.

After Colby finished his call, he made another one to his boss in Destiny.

"Chief Thornton? Yeah, it's Colby." He jerked the phone away from his ear, wincing.

Piper could hear the hooting and hollering going on, even from three feet away. "I take it your team is happy to hear from you."

"Apparently."

He winked, just like the old Colby. And she nearly melted into a puddle of gratitude to finally have him back. Hurt Colby, nearly drowned Colby, freezing-to-death Colby had all terrified her that he might pay the ultimate price just because he'd had the bad luck to have been dragged into her problems.

When the noise died down, he put the phone back to his ear. "Yes, sir, we're both okay. She's right here with me." He smiled at her again. "The short version is that Todd Palmer and some thugs of his kidnapped us and drove us up into the mountains in Johnson County." He listened for a moment, then he said to Piper, "The sheriff is sending someone to pick us up. It would be great if you could send them Palmer's driver's license photo so they can be on the lookout for him."

His smile slowly faded and his gaze shot to hers. "Yes, sir. Yes. Okay. You're certain?" He stepped closer to the desk, bending over an old-fashioned fax machine on top. "I'm on a landline actually. Neither of us has our cell phones. But there's a fax machine here. I'll give you the number."

He answered several more questions, giving them the basics about Jedidiah and his crew of miscreants and their escape, recapture, then release.

The fax machine whirred to life and a piece of paper slowly printed out of the top, curling like a scroll. Colby cradled the phone between his cheek and shoulder and used both hands to unravel the paper. But he was standing at an angle that didn't allow Piper to see what he was looking at.

"Yep. Got it...Blake and Dillon?...That would be great...I'll want to escort her home, so that works out perfectly...Uh-huh...Right...I understand. Thanks, Chief. Talk to you later."

He set the phone back on its base and turned with

the paper in his hands. It had curled up again, and he made no move to uncurl it.

"What was all that about?" she asked.

"For one thing, two of my teammates—Blake Sullivan and Dillon Gray—are heading out here to work with the Johnson County sheriff's office on the investigation into Palmer and Jedidiah. They're already actively searching for Palmer. When Gladiator didn't show up at Dillon's rescue farm, Griffin—his manager—notified Dillon, who called the fair just about the same time that a citizen called 911 to report that a deputy had stolen his gelding and hadn't returned it."

"You, when you came after me and Gladiator."

He nodded. "Unfortunately, that was a couple of hours after you and I were kidnapped. And it took a while to put enough pieces together to figure out what might have happened. They tried to contact Palmer, using the number he gave us, but no one answered. They started an investigation thinking something had happened to all three of us. Then Dillon requested driver's license photos of you and Palmer so he could put out a BOLO."

"BOLO?"

"'Be on the lookout.' It tells law enforcement to keep an eye out for a particular person or vehicle or both. When the pictures came back, he knew there was a problem." He pulled the paper straight and turned it around.

It was a grainy black-and-white picture of a white man, probably in his mid to late forties with a bald head and elaborate tattoos covering both of his beefy arms.

"Should I recognize him?" she asked.

His jaw tightened. "In theory, yes. It's Todd Palmer. The *real* one."

Chapter Thirteen

"We may not know the fake Palmer's true identity yet," Colby said. "But at least we have a lead on our mountain man." He slid a folder across the conference room table toward Dillon and Blake. "Seems he's had a few run-ins with the law around here. As soon as Piper and I described him, the sheriff knew exactly who we were talking about. His legal name is Daniel Jedidiah Holmes."

"He calls himself Jedidiah, not Daniel," Piper added from her seat beside Colby. She waved toward the food-filled table at the end of the glass-walled room. "Everyone in the sheriff's office has been super nice and helpful. There's coffee, soda, water, sandwiches, you name it."

Dillon shook his head. "Thank you but I'd rather dig into this case instead of food right now." He motioned toward the squad room visible through the glass. "Where is the sheriff? I didn't see him when the deputy ushered us in here a few minutes ago."

"He and a handful of his men are up on the mountain, searching for the body of Palmer's thug that I killed, and for Jedidiah," Colby told him. "I'm not holding out much hope that Jedidiah and his people stuck around. They probably grabbed what they could and hightailed it out of there right after they let us go."

Blake was nodding before he'd finished. "I've dealt with squatters and drifters before. They've usually got bags packed to leave at a moment's notice. Most of them are harmless."

"This one isn't." Dillon closed the file he'd been flipping through and handed it to Blake. "Looks like a real prince. This guy's been in trouble with the law since he was a juvenile. Mostly breaking and entering, trespassing, stealing cars. He's been in and out of prison a few times, the last time a few months ago. His family or crew or whatever he calls them must have been up on the mountain, waiting for him while he was in prison. I can't imagine that elaborate a setup, with all those outbuildings and that kitchen you described, being thrown together in just a couple of months. They've probably been squatting there for a long time."

"There's no history of violence here," Blake said, skimming through the pages in the folder. "Mainly he's a thief, but overall, harmless."

"He sure as hell isn't harmless," Colby gritted out.

Blake held up his hands. "Sorry. You're right. I was just interpreting what I saw on the rap sheet."

Dillon tapped the file on Todd Palmer that he'd brought with him. "We need to figure out the connection between Palmer, or whatever his real name is, and this Jedidiah fellow. You two mentioned that both Jedidiah and his daughter were familiar with his name. But neither appeared to like him, which could suggest they're enemies. If so, it makes sense that Palmer would drive all that way and dump you two on that particular mountain, knowing some cop-hating squatters lived there."

"You think he figured Jedidiah would finish us off if Palmer's own men didn't manage to do the job?" Colby asked.

"Possibly. He might have even wanted to blame your deaths on Jedidiah once your bodies were found. Again, assuming they know each other and there's bad blood between them."

"I think you're probably onto something. Why else would Palmer drive so far? There are other remote locations where he could have left us, much closer to Destiny."

"Where do the horses fit in?" Piper asked. At their blank looks, she said, "Sorry, I shouldn't butt into the investigation."

Colby put his hand on her shoulder. "Your input is just as valuable as anyone else's in this room. Don't apologize. The truck and trailer and a description of both horses is in the BOLO, right, Dillon?"

"Right. And we've extended the BOLO to the entire state. Your rig and that black stallion are both attention getters. Someone's bound to spot them and call them in."

The sick feeling in her stomach told her that if Gladiator was okay, someone would have seen him by now. She smiled her thanks.

"I think we should focus on Palmer and let the sheriff deal with Jedidiah," Colby said. "If we can figure out why Palmer chose that particular alias, it might help us get closer to figuring out his identity."

He picked up the picture that Dillon and Blake had brought with them, a sketch of Palmer. Although Destiny didn't have a sketch artist, they'd driven to a neighboring county that did and gave him their descriptions based on their encounters with Palmer at the fair.

Piper stared at the sketch in Colby's hands. It was eerily accurate. She rubbed her arms, feeling cold all over again.

"You okay?" Colby asked.

"Just…remembering." She looked at the other sketches of the men who'd been with Palmer, sketches made by the artist here a few hours earlier, based on her and Colby's recollections.

"No one is going to hurt you again, Piper. I won't let them."

She smiled, then noticed Dillon and Blake watching them closely. "Sorry, please, continue your discussion. You think there was a special reason Palmer chose to impersonate the real Todd Palmer?"

"Maybe," Dillon drawled, glancing back and forth between them. He rolled his shoulders as if to relieve some tension. "People tend to stick close to home, to places they're familiar with, when committing crimes. Palmer has been all over Tennessee these past few weeks. We've traced him to half a dozen fairs. And yet the man he impersonated was from Lexington, Kentucky, not that far from your place, Miss Caraway."

Colby absently tapped the table. "The alias came first, then the roaming around. I'd say he's from the Bluegrass State."

"I think so, too," Dillon agreed. "Probably spent at

least part of his formative years in or around Lexington. As for that alias, the address on the driver's license that he gave us matches the real Palmer's address. Only the picture is fake. What I don't get is why he didn't try to pick someone who at least bore a passing resemblance to him when choosing the alias in case anyone ever ran a search and pulled up the real Palmer's photo. It's almost like he was making some kind of joke, or thumbing his nose at law enforcement."

"Or he never expected to get caught and didn't worry about the photo," Blake said.

"Maybe." Dillon didn't sound convinced.

"Whatever the reason," Colby said, "just the fact that he impersonated a man from Lexington is enough for me to vote that we extend that BOLO to Lexington and the surrounding counties."

"Agreed." Dillon motioned to Blake.

Blake headed out of the room, presumably to modify the BOLO again.

As soon as the door closed, Colby asked, "Are Blake and Donna still at each other's throats after the chief assigned Donna to mentor him?"

Dillon rolled his eyes. "Like you wouldn't believe."

"Wait," Piper said. "Donna? The officer I met at the fair? I thought they were a couple."

Both men laughed.

"That's rich," Colby said. "Donna's going to love hearing that." He chuckled again. "Donna's a peacemaker, gets along with everybody and their brother. Blake, on the other hand, is like a burr under a saddle. He rubs everyone the wrong way. Out of desperation, our boss assigned Donna as his partner, to show him the ropes and help him get more acclimated to how we do things in Destiny. He's former military and then was a detective in Knoxville before joining our squad. He's still clinging to his old ways, but we'll bring him around."

"If we don't kill him first," Dillon grumbled.

Piper wasn't sure if he was kidding or not. She'd definitely noticed tension between the two since they'd arrived. "He and Donna seemed to be getting along well at the fair."

Dillon shook his head. "Looks can be deceiving. There's a reason Donna begged for me to come up here instead of her. Originally, the chief wanted those two to make the drive while I stayed behind to keep things going in Destiny. But Donna said unless they wanted to bring Blake back in a body bag, that the chief had better assign someone else to go with him. I drew the short straw."

"Gee, thanks," Colby said.

Dillon grinned. "Nothing personal. But I've got a gorgeous wife and new baby at home waiting for me. Traveling as part of the job isn't nearly the fun it used to be. Even if it's to help a fellow officer and friend."

Colby smiled. "I can understand that." His replacement cell phone buzzed in his pocket and he pulled it out to look at the screen. "They've found the body of the man I stabbed up on the mountain. No identity yet but they're scanning his prints. No sign of Jedidiah's camp yet either. The CSI guys are going to process the spot where Palmer left us while the sheriff and his men continue the search for Jedidiah."

Blake came back into the room and sat at the table.

"I expanded the BOLO and spoke to Sheriff Jamie O'Leary of Meadow County, your county, Miss Caraway. One of his men was near the real Todd Palmer's place when I called and went ahead and checked on him. He wasn't there but a neighbor vouched for him, said he's out of state on an extended trip trying to drum up new customers for his business. The neighbor spoke to him just this morning and said Todd's fine and not expected back for a few more weeks. Apparently, that's no secret around town either."

Colby scrubbed the stubble on his chin. He and Piper had been treated to fresh clothes and new phones, courtesy of a sheriff-paid trip to Walmart, and the use of showers at a local motel after they'd first arrived. But he hadn't taken the time to shave. He'd been too anxious to get to the police station and dig into the investigation. Piper would have preferred to get some sleep at the motel, but she didn't want to be there alone and miss anything either.

"Maybe that's why the fake Palmer chose that alias," Colby said. "He didn't have to worry about the real guy being around. Which means he probably does come from Lexington like we thought, and whatever clandestine business he's doing, he expects to be done in the next few weeks before the real Palmer returns."

"The only other connection to Lexington is the Caraway ranch, and you, Miss Caraway," Dillon said. "Are you positive you've never seen fake Palmer before?" He tapped the picture on the table.

"Honestly, there's nothing at all familiar about him. I've never met the real Palmer either."

"But our guy met her parents," Colby said. "Based

on some things that he said, it seems like he must have met them. And they passed away about ten years ago."

"My condolences," Dillon said.

"Thank you. It's been a long time."

"That doesn't mean the pain goes away. I lost my sister when I was in college and she was still in high school. I know it sticks with you." He awkwardly cleared his throat. "As for this case's connection to that horse of yours, Gladiator, did you get a chance to text that police artist sketch of Palmer to your ranch manager?"

"Actually, no. After our little shopping trip this morning for clothes and replacement phones, I called Billy. But that was just to let him know I was okay since I hadn't checked in with him in a few days. I also had to tell him that Gladiator was missing and to postpone any upcoming stud service appointments until we know if he's…" She cleared her throat. "Until we know whether we'll get him back. I'll text him a picture of the sketch you brought with you. It's a lot better than the one the artist here rendered for Colby and me."

She snapped a picture of the sketch, then typed a text message and hit Send. A few seconds later, they had their reply. Billy confirmed that the man he'd given Gladiator to was indeed the man in their sketch.

"Not that there was much of a question at this point," Colby said, "but it's good to have confirmation. So we're back to why did he choose Piper's ranch, why Gladiator and why did he want to kill Piper?"

"And you," she added.

He shook his head. "No. None of this points to me. I was just in the way. It all seems to center around you."

"I have to agree," Blake added. "We need more background on you and your family, including the business that you run." He grabbed a pen and a legal pad from a stack on the table. "If Palmer knew your parents, then he was in the area ten-plus years ago. You said you left after they died. When did you come back?"

She frowned. "Well, I came back to the ranch as soon as I legally could, after I turned eighteen. I loved my aunt Helen, but I wanted to go home and take over the running of the business from Billy."

Dillon's head snapped up from the notes he'd been writing. "Your manager ran the business alone until you came back?"

"For the most part. He sent reports to my aunt and she approved expenditures over a certain amount and reviewed any contracts, but overall, yes, he ran things. Why?"

"How long was he in charge?"

"Aunt Helen hired him after my parents' car accident. So, I guess about four or five years. But I've been overseeing it for the past six years and hired him back as my assistant once I realized I needed help. If you think he resents me being in charge, you're wrong. Billy's as easygoing as they come. And if he had any issues with me, I'd have seen some kind of evidence long before now."

"You're probably right. Still, we need to look into this Billy guy. Last name?"

"Abbott." She spelled it and he wrote it down.

"Okay," Blake said. "Someone mentioned earlier that you've never seen Palmer. So that means he was out of the picture for the past six years at least. But a few months ago he shows up with the fraudulent paperwork and steals your horse, while you're out of town." He tapped his pencil on his tablet. "I'm not sure whether he wanted you to find him or not. But regardless, he had hired muscle to deal with you—and the policeman who inconveniently got in the way—without having to scramble for a backup plan. He was prepared ahead of time. That's not the hallmark of a rookie. He's more than likely a career criminal. And I can think of only one reason a career criminal would disappear for several years, then suddenly show up again."

"Prison," Colby and Dillon both said at the same time.

"And now he's on parole, or he served his whole term and is out for good," Colby added. "Assuming that he really did disappear and wasn't just around somewhere else and Piper didn't happen to see him. But that's a good working theory. We could check into any prisoner releases in Kentucky about two months ago, convicts who match Palmer's description."

"I'm on it. I'll check prisons in Tennessee, too, just in case," Blake said and headed out of the room again.

Piper blinked at the closing door. "He's certainly energetic, hopping in and out of the room all the time to research things."

Dillon snorted. "He's just glad for an excuse to get away from me."

Colby grinned and looked at Piper. "Didn't you tell me earlier that your ranch was going great up until a few months ago? That you were even planning on expanding, building a new stable?"

"Adding on to our existing stables, yes. The stables are in great shape even though they're eight or nine years old. They're at the edge of the property, on a tract of land my father sold to my neighbor—Mr. Wilkerson—back when I was still in middle school. At the time, Mr. Wilkerson had a booming breeding business and wanted the land for grazing. But then my parents died and I was sent to Paducah to live with my aunt. And while I was gone, Mrs. Wilkerson died of cancer and Mr. Wilkerson sold off his horses and quit the business."

She waved her hand. "Sorry, I'm getting to the point, which is that once I came back and was running the ranch and things were going well, I bought the land back from Mr. Wilkerson to expand. The nearly new state-of-the-art stables were built on that parcel right before his wife got sick. He put his whole life on hold to care for her and never even used the stables. They sat empty and were in pristine condition. When I offered to buy the land with the stables, he made a counteroffer with a much lower price."

"Lower?" Colby shook his head. "Why would he do that?"

"I think he just wanted to get rid of everything having to do with the business. And he decided to give me the same price that he'd originally paid for the land from my dad. Maybe he thought he was doing me a favor or honoring my father, I don't know. I argued with him, believe me. But in the end, he gave me an ultimatum to take the deal or forget it. I took the deal."

"What do stables cost?" Colby asked. "Are we talking an insane amount of money here?"

She felt her face flush with heat. "I don't know about insane, but it's in the hundreds of thousands of dollars."

Dillon exchanged a quick glance with Colby before looking at her again. "Does Wilkerson have a family? Someone who might resent him making that deal, essentially foregoing money that could have fattened their inheritance?"

She shook her head. "Not that I know of. He and his wife never had any children. I remember Mom saying that Mrs. Wilkerson was an only child, that her parents had died a long time back. Mr. Wilkerson had a sister or brother, but they were estranged. The only reason that I know he had a sibling is because his nephew visited them one summer for a few weeks. I think his name was Dwayne or something like that. But it's not like our families were close or we were always watching the road out front. Even though they're neighbors, I can only see their house from the stables on our land. So there could have been other relatives who visited that we never knew about." She shook her head again. "Sorry. I know I'm not much help."

"You're doing great," Colby said. "Tell me more about the stables. You said they weren't big enough once your business started booming, so you planned on expanding. But you said you had to cancel your plans to add on, because of the mishaps?"

"Mishaps?" Dillon rested his forearms on the table. "What does that mean?"

She sighed. "The sheriff in my county already had some of his deputies look into those things. Nothing raised any red flags for him. It's just that a lot of accidents have been happening—equipment breaking down, things getting lost. It forced me to dip into savings, big-time. And with the expansion plans and payments I already made to contractors to get on their construction schedules, I ran out of liquid cash and couldn't pay the mortgage. That's why I left before Gladiator was taken. I went to an auction to sell a few of my top horses so I could pay the mortgage and make payroll, just to tide us over until things got better." She shook her head. "Unfortunately, the horses didn't fetch as high a price as I needed and I was still short on the mortgage. Then I found out about Gladiator and, well, you know the rest. I really need to get home soon so I can figure out how to plug the hole in my sinking financial ship."

Dillon looked like he was about to ask another question but a knock sounded on the door. At Dillon's wave, a deputy poked his head inside the room. "Got a minute?"

"What's up?" Dillon asked.

He stepped inside, leading a young white man, dressed in a gray T-shirt and faded jeans.

"This is Derrick Huff. Tell them what you told me, Mr. Huff."

The man, who couldn't have been more than twenty, looked extremely nervous as he fingered a piece of rumpled notebook paper in his hands.

"Go on," the deputy urged.

Instead of saying anything, Huff handed the paper to Colby, who was the closest to the door.

Colby frowned and started reading the paper, then shot out of his chair. "You're with Jedidiah? Where is he?"

Huff's eyes widened like round moons. "No, no, no. I'm not with anyone. A guy stopped me a few blocks down the road and offered me money if I'd—"

"Deputy, send some men to—"

The deputy held up his hands. "It's already handled, Detective Vale. We have some officers canvassing the street, looking for Jedidiah." He put his hand on Huff's shoulders. "Just tell them what happened."

"Like...like I said. This guy stopped me a few blocks away and paid me to drive his truck over here and give you that note."

Piper stood beside Colby, trying to read the paper.

"What's it say?" Dillon's face was lined with impatience.

Colby frowned at Huff as if he wanted to arrest him. But he read the note out loud.

"I know this Palmer guy you mentioned to Mindy. All I'll say on that is he's bad news. Once you left the mountain—"

"Left?" Piper exclaimed. "Did he really say we left, like we were just up there for a visit? He kidnapped us!" Everyone was looking at her. She felt her face flush with heat. "Sorry. Go on. Finish reading the note."

Colby gave her a reassuring smile, then continued.

"—we went looking for Palmer and his men to make sure they weren't close by where they could hurt someone. We found the truck and trailer you were looking for, off in a ditch a few miles away—with the horses still inside. Abandoned. It looked like it hit a patch of ice and slid off the road and Palmer and his men didn't even bother to try to save the horses."

Piper covered her mouth with her hands.

Colby's face flushed with anger and he handed the note to Dillon, then pulled Piper into his arms. "I'm sorry, Piper. I'm so sorry about Gladiator."

Dillon scanned the rest of the note. "Doesn't say much else, just that he wanted to return what was rightfully yours and he's sorry for everything that happened." He shook his head. "Obviously he's trying to backtrack to make it easier on himself once he's arrested."

Piper fought hard to hold back her tears. It was only because of Colby's strong arms around her that she was able to cling to her composure.

"So where are the truck and trailer?" Colby asked Huff.

"Out front, in the parking lot." He pulled a set of keys from his pocket and held them out.

"Drop them on the table. We'll have someone go over it for prints. Who knows. Maybe Palmer was dumb enough to leave a perfect set and we can run it through AFIS and get a match."

Piper shook her head. "I don't think we'll get that lucky."

"Probably not."

Huff frowned in confusion and glanced from the deputy to Colby. "But what are you going to do about the horses? It's cold outside. And they need food and water."

Piper jerked her head up. "Food and water?"

"They're alive?" Colby asked.

"Well, yeah. A red one and a huge black one. Don't think I've ever seen one like that before. What kind—"

Piper shoved past him and ran out of the conference room.

Chapter Fourteen

Dillon waved toward the cache of weapons in the open trunk of Blake's car outside the Johnson County sheriff's office. "You sure that's all you want to take?"

Colby shoved the pistol that Dillon had just given him into the holster clipped to his belt. "I've got four magazines in my jacket pockets and one in the gun. If I need more ammo than that, I'm toast."

"Good point." Dillon grinned. "You know, you could let Miss Caraway drive that horse of hers back to her ranch by herself while you stay here with Blake and me and gather evidence on Jedidiah and his crew. The three of us can head up to Lexington in the morning to coordinate with the sheriff up there and find out what we can about Palmer. No need for you to crash in Miss Caraway's guest room tonight when you can bunk with us at a nice hotel in Mountain City."

Dillon glanced toward Piper fifty yards away, who was grilling the large animal vet with questions even though Gladiator had already been examined and given the all clear to go home. The gelding wasn't as lucky. He was dehydrated and would remain in the doctor's care until he deemed the horse well enough to travel back to Destiny to be reunited with its owner. But in spite of the reassurances, Piper was still asking the poor doctor questions even while he loaded the gelding into the trailer that he'd brought.

"Piper assured me she didn't mind me using the guest room for tonight. She even offered for all three of us to stay as long as we're in Lexington. But I told her we'd get a hotel once you two come up. If I thought you and Blake really needed me today, I'd stay. But I know you don't. And I can't sit in a conference room while Piper's making a five-hour trek, all alone, in that rig of hers. She's been through a terrible ordeal. And that checkup by an EMT when we got here was a joke. I think she needs time to rest and recuperate. I want to drive her home and make sure she gets there okay."

"You went through the same ordeal and are recovering from a concussion. I imagine you're just as tired."

At Colby's frown, Dillon laughed and clapped him on the shoulder. "I knew it. You've been bitten by the bug, my friend. I can't wait to tell Ashley. She'll be thrilled."

"What bug?"

"The love bug."

Colby shoved him. Hard. Which only made Dillon laugh harder.

His smile faded and he turned serious. "All teasing aside, if you run into any trouble along the way or after you get there, Blake and me can be there in a couple of hours on the sheriff's chopper. I mean it. If things go sideways, call me."

Colby nodded. "I will. Thanks."

"We'll finish up here tonight and head to Lexington in the morning. I haven't had a chance to set up an appointment with the sheriff there yet—"

"I did," Colby said. "Called him before you two arrived. He's expecting us in his office around one. I already briefed him on the case, too, and he said he'd send a deputy to the ranch to check things out."

Dillon nodded his approval. "You're making my job too easy. Next I know, you'll want to be lead detective."

"Nah. The pay's not good enough for the extra headaches."

"Ha, no kidding."

"Dillon." Blake's voice rang out. He was standing in the open doorway to the building. "The sheriff's on the phone for you."

Dillon clapped Colby on the shoulder. "We'll see you around lunchtime tomorrow, if not before."

"Sounds good."

Dillon jogged back to the building.

Colby waved to Blake then strode to the horse trailer. Piper was exhausted—so exhausted that she was sleeping, standing up with the truck's keys dangling perilously from one of her fingers. Her mouth was slightly parted and she was slumped half against the wheel well. He was just about to shake her awake when her eyes flew open.

She let out a cry of alarm and swung her fist toward his jaw.

He ducked out of the way. "Hey, hey, Piper. It's me, Colby. It's okay. You're safe."

She froze, then recognition flooded her eyes and she gasped in horror.

"Colby. I'm so sorry."

"No worries. You didn't hit me."

She grimaced. "Did I...fall asleep? Standing up?"

"Yep." He snagged the keys. "Looks like you've been around your horses a bit too much. You're taking on their characteristics. Personally, I prefer sleeping in a bed over standing up."

"Ha, ha." She covered her mouth as she yawned. "Good grief. I really am tired."

"Which is why I'm driving. Come on. Let's get you settled into the cab." He started to lead her to the passenger side, half expecting her to fall over because she was so tired. But she suddenly stopped.

"Wait, Palmer kept my purse or threw it out after he stole my truck. I don't have my license or credit cards and this thing is a gas guzzler. We'll never make it to Lexington on one tank."

"No worries." He gently pulled her to the passenger side and opened the door. "I've got a Destiny PD credit card, courtesy of Dillon. And I printed out copies of our licenses from our respective DMVs until we can both get new ones."

"I'm impressed. You thought of everything."

"Not quite." He lifted her up into the cab, noting the attractive blush that spread across her cheeks before he let her go.

She cleared her throat. "What did you forget?"

"I didn't forget exactly. But I haven't had a chance to take care of something that's bothering me." He held up the ring full of keys. "I know Palmer expected us to die on that mountain, so it's unlikely he copied your keys. But do you think one of your ranch hands can get the locks changed on your house before you get home?"

She looked down. "Of course. Thanks. I can call Billy and he'll—"

He gently tilted her head up. "Piper..." A single tear tracked down her cheek.

She pushed his hand away and swiped at the tear. "I'm fine. Just... I'm tired is all."

He cupped her face in his hands until she looked at him. "You're the bravest, strongest person I know. But even a brave person needs to cry it out sometimes. And that's okay, too. It's okay, sweetheart."

Her face crumpled, and then she was reaching for him, or he was reaching for her; he wasn't sure which. But he stood in the open doorway with her arms around his neck, his arms around her waist, holding her tight. And nothing had ever felt so right.

Normally, a crying woman would make him want to run the other way in panic. But not with Piper. The heartbreaking sobs shaking her petite frame only made him want to hold her tighter and protect her and make sure nothing bad ever happened to her again.

Somehow the words she needed to hear in that moment found their way to his lips, and he whispered them into her hair as he rocked her against him. And when the tears stopped and the storm passed, another storm took its place. Her mouth brushed against his skin at the V of his shirt and sent a rush of adrenaline pumping through his body. He tensed, his breath catching in his throat. Desire slammed into him like a hurricane, flooding his senses, making him shake with the intensity.

Piper drew back, her face flushed with heat, her own breaths coming fast and hard as she stared at his lips. Then her pink tongue darted out and he almost died right then and there.

"Colby," she whispered, pulling him toward her, angling her mouth up.

A ragged breath escaped between his clenched teeth. He wanted to lean down, meet her halfway. But it wasn't right. She was half-asleep, scared, vulnerable. And he wasn't in much better shape himself. Plus, he was afraid that if he ever kissed her again, he wouldn't be able to stop.

It almost killed him, but he pulled back and tugged her arms down. At the questioning look on her face, he tried to smile, but was pretty sure he failed miserably. "We shouldn't. Not now. Not here."

She blinked as if shocked to realize where they were. "What was I thinking?" She pushed him back. "Go on. I'll call Billy, get those locks changed. I guess I'm more tired than I realized. I'm doing crazy things." She gave an embarrassed laugh and punched a number into her phone as she pulled the door shut.

He stood outside her door for a full minute while he tried to regain control. Meanwhile, she finished her call and clicked her seat belt, all without looking at him.

He'd embarrassed her and he hated that. Did she think he didn't want her? That he'd pulled away because he wasn't interested? Nothing could be further from the truth. Even now his pulse was slamming through his veins, rushing through his ears. He wanted her with an intensity that was alarming.

He headed to the driver's side. Somehow he had to figure out how to make this right. He didn't want her embarrassed and thinking he wasn't attracted to her.

He hopped into the driver's seat, started the engine, then looked over at her.

She was asleep.

He grinned and shook his head. So much for worrying about hurting her feelings.

About an hour later, he was rounding a curve on a rural two-lane highway when a warm hand touched his on the steering wheel. He glanced at Piper and smiled. "Hey, sleepyhead."

"Pull over."

He frowned. "What?"

"You heard me. Pull over."

"Is something—"

"Colby."

"Okay, okay." He pulled to the side of the highway, halfway on the winter-brown grass to make sure no one would hit them. Then he put the truck into Park. "What's wrong?"

"I need you to kiss me."

His mouth went dry. "Sorry. What?"

"Just do it, okay? Kiss me. It's an experiment."

"An experiment?" He felt like an idiot repeating everything she said, but he was so dumbfounded by her request that he couldn't quite make sense of it.

She unclipped her seat belt, got on her knees on the seat beside him and leaned over, crushing her breasts against his chest. "Kiss. Me."

His gaze fell to her lips, then lower, where her shirt gaped open, revealing the delectable cleavage he'd tried, in vain, to push out of his mind ever since she'd taken off her bra up in the mountain.

"Piper, you don't know what you're asking. You're still exhausted, traumatized—"

She pressed her lips to his and destroyed every ounce of honor he had left. His conscience evaporated beneath the tantalizing heat of her mouth, the erotic tug of her teeth against his lips as she tried to coax him to kiss her back.

He groaned deep in his throat and pulled her onto his lap, straddling him with her delicious heat. Sliding one hand down the arch of her back, he caressed her backside and drove his other hand deep into the luxurious fall of her hair, desperate to pull her even closer. He drank her in, their tongues dueling, tasting, teasing until he was aching with the pleasure-pain of wanting her, wanting…more.

Their kisses in the mountain had been born of a desperation to survive, to generate heat, to chase away the fog of delirium. This kiss was born of a consuming fascination that had sparked to life the instant he'd seen her at the fair, tiny yet spunky and brave, risking everything for the love of a horse. His desire for her had been simmering ever since, and now that it had broken free, it scorched both of them, consuming them from the inside out.

He half turned with her, pressing her against the door. He wanted to kiss her…everywhere…but not yet. Not until he had her screaming his name from just a regular kiss. Not that this was like any kiss he'd ever experienced. Good grief, the woman was like one of those sexy sirens of old folklore. Where had she learned to kiss like this? That thought sent an insane spark of jealousy straight through him. He suddenly wanted to kill any man who'd ever dared to look at her. As he made love to her mouth with his, one word kept repeating itself over and over in his lust-fogged brain.

Mine.

The shock of what that word meant sent a cold chill through his body and cleared the fog of passion that had gripped him like a prisoner. He broke the kiss, pushing her back, his lungs straining for oxygen.

Her luscious breasts rose and fell with her own ragged breaths, taunting him, tempting him to kiss her again.

"No." His voice was a husky rasp. He cleared his throat.

She blinked, the passion clouding her eyes beginning to fade, as well. "No?"

He closed his eyes, drew another deep breath, then looked at her again. "I'm sorry. This isn't right. You're vulnerable right now and not thinking straight, and I…"

"You… What?" She studied him for a moment, then scrambled off his lap and plopped down on the seat beside him. "You don't want me?"

He laughed harshly and waved toward his lap. "I think the answer to that is obvious." He scrubbed his face and grasped the steering wheel as if it were an anchor and it could save him from being tossed out to sea. "I want you more than… Hell, I want you more than I've ever wanted anyone. But it's a hundred different ways of wrong."

"Why?"

She didn't sound angry or hurt now. She sounded curious, like she was thinking through a problem. How could she act like her world hadn't tilted when his had turned completely upside down and inside out. Was that the experiment she'd mentioned? Had she wanted to toy with him and see what happened? The passion that had boiled through him moments ago shifted. Frustration, hurt and anger warred inside him. His hands clenched around the steering wheel.

"Did you get what you wanted?"

She blinked. "What?"

"You said you were conducting an experiment. What was the point? See if I was a jerk who'd take advantage of a woman when she was vulnerable? Well, you got your answer. I'm scum."

"What? No, no, no, no. Colby, I just needed to know if those kisses in the mountain were just about keeping warm, or whether you feel the same—" she licked her lips, her gaze dropping to his mouth "—heat, that I do, every time I look at you."

Her tongue darted out to wet her lips again and his traitorous body jerked in response. Lust flared through him again. He swore.

She shoved her hair back from her face. "You've got deep roots in Destiny, don't you? I don't guess you'd ever want to move away."

He let out a deep breath. He was tired, so tired. His head still hurt from all the knocks he'd taken. That was the only explanation for him thinking, for even a second, that Piper had been playing with him. She wasn't the mean, vindictive type. And he was taking his own frustrations out on her.

"No," he said, in a much calmer tone this time. "I wouldn't." Disappointment ripped through him as the truth of her words sank in, and what that meant for their future together. Or lack of one. "And you've got deep roots in that ranch of yours. I don't see you wanting to give up your family legacy to live in Destiny."

"No. I wouldn't."

They stared at each other a full minute, neither of them blinking as a world of emotion and thoughts swirled between them. Neither of them needed to say anything. They'd just said it all. They desired each other like crazy, and yet there was no way for them to be together. They had completely different goals, and neither of them was willing to give that up.

He should have stayed in Mountain City with Dillon and Blake.

She clicked her seat belt and turned to look out the window. "Take me home please."

He stared at her, wanting to heal the hurt that pulsed between them like a living thing. But what could he say? They'd known each other for a few days. This… whatever it was…between them wasn't enough to give up everything either of them had ever wanted, enough to completely change their lives.

There was no healing, no magic thing he could say to make it better. The best he could do now was get her home and settled so she could go on with her life and forget him.

But how the hell was *he* ever going to forget *her*?

Chapter Fifteen

The five-hour drive from the Johnson County sheriff's office to Piper's ranch an hour outside Lexington would have been agonizingly awkward after that disastrous "experiment" with Colby, except that Piper had been exhausted and slept through most of it. When they finally drove under the "Caraway Ranch" archway and headed up the long gravel road to her house, she almost wept with relief.

Until she saw what was waiting for her. Then she wanted to weep for an entirely different reason.

Colby slowed the truck. "This can't be good. I wonder why the sheriff's at your house."

"The usual, I imagine. Another disaster of some kind that he's looking into. Probably the same disaster that explains the moat in the left-side yard and the plumber's truck. They charge a fortune by the hour, don't they? I wonder if I have to pay for his drive time on top of any repairs. If so, I'm out two hours of labor costs just for the drive from town and back."

As soon as he parked the truck and trailer behind the police cruiser, she reached for the door handle. But Colby stopped her with a hand on her shoulder.

"Piper, I make a decent chunk of money from my farm on top of my salary. I've got a healthy nest egg in the bank. I could give you—"

"No." She winced. "Sorry, but I don't want to take your money or anyone else's. I'll figure something out. Thanks for the offer. I do appreciate it."

She reached for the handle again, then stared in stunned amazement as the front door of her home opened and three people stepped out, one of them in handcuffs.

"Who's the girl being arrested? Do you know her?"

"I thought I did. Apparently, I don't know her that well at all if she's been arrested. Her name is Arlene Garza. She's a ranch hand I hired a couple of months ago."

The deputy put the girl in the back seat, then shut the door.

"And the guy with the deputy?" Colby asked.

"Billy Abbott. My ranch manager. Come on, I'll introduce you and see what's going on."

They both hopped out of the truck and met the others beside the patrol car.

"Piper, it's so good to see you." Billy pulled her into a tight hug.

"Can't. Breathe," she teased.

He let her go, his face turning red. "Sorry. I'm just so glad you're okay." He looked toward the trailer and his face lit with a grin. "Thank goodness you found Gladiator. But, oh, wow, I'm so sorry I screwed up. That bill of sale looked legit and you weren't answering your phone and I wasn't sure what to do and—"

"Hold it, stop. Stop. We've already gone over that.

It's in the past, okay? Now, what's going on here? Why is Arlene in handcuffs?"

The young girl was crying in the back seat. Even through the car's rear window, Piper could see her shoulders shaking. Beside the car, Colby was in deep conversation with the deputy.

"Well?" Piper asked. "What's going on? And why is my yard flooded?"

Billy's hands fisted beside him. "We've had a few more pieces of equipment go missing, and one of the saddles was found soaking in a trough. It's completely ruined. I was so frustrated I went into town and bought one of those game cameras, the kind hunters use that only snap pictures when someone moves."

Piper was still reeling from the news about the saddle being ruined, then she realized what he'd said about the camera. All she could see were dollar signs as she tried to imagine how much something like that had cost her. She had no idea.

"When I came up from the stables a few hours ago, I found the yard the way you see it now, only worse. Water was gushing from a broken water spigot on the other side of the house. I had to turn off the water to the whole house to get it off. The valve at the spigot was broken. Thankfully, the plumber was able to fix it pretty quick. But I asked him to check the rest of the plumbing out to make sure no one sabotaged anything else."

"Sabotage. So it was Arlene? You're sure?"

"She admitted it. And even if she hadn't, I've got proof." He waved toward one of the trees about fifty yards from the front of the house. "I put the camera there after the saddle incident. And I checked the SD card inside it after I got the water turned off. There are some perfect shots of Arlene taking a baseball bat to that spigot. I called the sheriff right after I called the plumber."

She shook her head. "I don't understand why she would do something like that. She seemed like such a sweet girl. What does she have to gain?"

Colby and the deputy stopped in front of them.

The deputy shook her hand. "Miss Caraway, I'm Deputy Hollenbeck. So far Miss Garza isn't talking. But based on what Detective Vale told me about the Palmer guy, I'm betting she's working with him and is the person behind all the vandalism you've been experiencing."

"Wait. You're saying she's behind everything that's happened? And that Palmer put her up to it?"

Hollenbeck nodded.

Colby shrugged. "We don't know all the facts yet. She's only admitted to busting the spigot but wouldn't say why. You said you hired a security guy a few months ago, too?"

"Ken Taylor. He's a friend of the sheriff. No way is he involved. I trust him completely."

"Did you trust Arlene completely?"

She frowned.

The door to the house opened and an older man in blue coveralls stepped out writing on what looked like an invoice book. Great.

Colby shot her a sympathetic look and moved back to give her some privacy. Her face flushed with heat.

His pity over her financial situation was the last thing that she wanted from him.

As the deputy pulled away in the patrol car, she turned to Billy. "Would you mind getting Gladiator settled into the stables for me?"

"Of course. By the way, I restocked your groceries and even went to Bradford's. Got your favorite—brisket. Wasn't sure what your, um, friend would want, so I got a full rack of baby back ribs with all the fixings. Everything's in the fridge."

"Thanks. I really appreciate it. My mouth's already watering over the brisket." She smiled and tossed him the keys, then waved Colby over to join them.

"Billy, meet my *friend*," she teased, "Detective Colby Vale. Colby, this is Billy Abbott, my right-hand man around here."

Billy flushed at the compliment and shook Colby's hand. "Piper said on the phone that you're from Tennessee. I wouldn't think a detective from Tennessee would have jurisdiction here in Kentucky."

"I drove Piper here as a courtesy and I'm assisting local law enforcement with the investigation. Don't worry. I'm not breaking any laws," he said drily.

Piper didn't think Billy's face could get redder if he'd been out in the sun all summer without sunscreen.

Billy awkwardly cleared his throat and waved toward the trailer. "Well, thank you for everything you did to save my boss, and our prize horse."

Colby narrowed his eyes, clearly studying Billy as if he thought he might turn into an ax murderer any second. "I can't take the credit. There was a lot of luck involved. And one of the bad guys ended up bringing Gladiator back for us."

"Oh. Well, to hear Piper tell it, you saved her life a gazillion times and if it weren't for you she'd have never made it. You have my gratitude."

"Will that be cash or credit?" a voice called out.

They all turned toward the plumber, who held up the invoice for Piper. She groaned when she saw the number of zeroes.

"Credit," she grumbled. "If I have any left. Let's go back inside." She stepped to the house and held the door open. "Colby? You coming?"

He looked back at Billy, who was getting in the truck. "I think I'll catch a ride to the stables if you don't mind. I'd like to meet that security guy of yours."

Billy paused at the driver's door, his face going pale at the idea of having Colby as a passenger.

"Is Ken at the stables right now?" she asked.

"As far as I know, he is."

"Great. Let's go." Colby hopped into the passenger seat and shut the door.

"Go on." Piper waved at Billy. "I'll head up there in the golf cart as soon as I can."

He nodded unenthusiastically and got into the truck.

"Miss Caraway? The bill?" the plumber reminded her.

"My office is to the right." She led the way into the house.

By the time she'd dealt with the plumber and a few minor emergencies that some other ranch hands brought her way, Colby and Billy had been gone for close to an hour. Surprised that Colby hadn't returned, she hopped onto the golf cart she kept parked beside the house—thankfully on the side that hadn't flooded—and headed toward the stables.

She pulled up just as Billy was loading one of the Thoroughbred stallions into the trailer that Gladiator had been in earlier.

"Billy? What's going on?"

He closed the back door of the trailer, securing the horse inside. "With the Arlene situation and the plumber here, I haven't had a chance to update you about ranch business. The bank came out while you were gone and gave us an ultimatum—pay the missed mortgage payments, plus interest and fees, immediately, or they would begin the foreclosure process. They threatened to get an injunction that would close down the ranch and take all the horses as assets until everything was settled."

She pressed her hand to her chest. "Good grief. I know we're behind, but that seems drastic. When does it have to be paid?"

"A week ago."

She blinked. "What? Then, wait, I don't understand." She looked toward the stables. "Oh, no. Are all the other horses—"

He held up a hand to stop her. "Relax. The mortgage is current. No one took any of the horses. Thanks to this guy." He waved toward the trailer. "My pimping skills have come in handy. Romeo here has two breeding appointments, both paid in advance."

"In advance? Two? Wow, way to go." She gave him a high five, then hugged him. "You're awesome. Thank you so much."

He gave her a funny look. "Don't act so surprised. I was running this ranch for years before you came back. I do know a thing or two about breeding."

She frowned. Had she offended him? "I didn't mean to—"

"I've gotta go before our clients demand their money back. I'll be gone for a couple of weeks. All the details are in the logbook in your office." He hopped into the driver's seat.

Piper ran to his window and tapped on it.

He rolled it down, his brows arching in question.

"Colby—Detective Vale, where is he?"

He pointed past the stables to the only house close to her property, about a hundred yards away, past the line of white three-rail fencing that surrounded her land.

"He's at Mr. Wilkerson's. Said he wanted to talk to him. I told Vale that the sheriff already interviewed Wilkerson after he came home a couple of days ago. But Vale headed over there anyway."

"How did the sheriff know that Mr. Wilkerson was back?"

"I called O'Leary the second I saw our neighbor out in his yard."

"Thanks. I probably don't say it often enough, but I really appreciate everything you do for me."

He gave her an embarrassed nod, never one for being comfortable with praise.

She stepped back and waited until the truck and trailer were safely on the road in front of the ranch. Then she drew a deep breath and headed toward her neighbor's house.

"You're sure you don't recognize this man?" Colby scooted forward on the couch and fanned out his copies of the police artist sketches on the coffee table. He smoothed the lines in one of them from having been folded up in his pocket. It was the picture of Palmer. He picked it up and held it out toward the older man.

Wilkerson didn't even look at it. "I've already spoken to the sheriff about this."

"Yes, sir. But Sheriff O'Leary didn't have these when you spoke to him a few days ago."

"Drawings that you've already shown me. I don't know anyone named Palmer and I had nothing to do with whatever nonsense is going on next door with that big black horse."

A knock sounded on the glass door off the back of the house. Piper stood there, waving at them.

Wilkerson let out a heavy sigh and laboriously pushed himself to his feet. "I've had more nosy visitors in the last week than I've had all year. Makes a man want to pack up and move."

Colby rolled his eyes behind the man and followed him to the door.

Wilkerson offered Piper the same frown he'd been gifting Colby with for the past ten minutes.

"Miss Caraway, if you're here for your detective fellow, you're welcome to him. He was just leaving. Goodbye, Detective."

"Thank you for your time." Colby reluctantly stepped outside.

The door slammed closed and Wilkerson drew the curtains.

Piper blinked. "Wow. What did you do to him?"

"Asked him a few questions. I think he's hiding something."

"Seriously?"

"Seriously." He stepped past her and headed across the gently rolling hill toward the fence he'd hopped earlier.

Piper fell in step beside him. "I'm sure he told you that he had nothing to do with the fake bill of sale. Billy told me a few minutes ago that the sheriff already spoke to Wilkerson about what happened."

He stopped at the fence and rested his arm across the top rail. "Your manager's close to your age isn't he? I think you said he was just out of high school when he started working at your ranch."

She frowned. "Billy? Yeah, he's about five years older than me. Why?"

"Billy Boy has a major crush on you."

Her face flushed a light pink. "I know that. It makes things…awkward sometimes since the feeling definitely isn't mutual." She waved her hand. "That's not relevant. Why did you talk to Mr. Wilkerson without me?"

Part of him wanted to warn her that she should set Billy straight, make sure he knew there was no future for him with Piper. But since he wasn't sure his dislike of the guy was because of some sixth sense about his character, or whether he was just plain jealous, he decided to keep his mouth shut about Billy. Instead, he answered her question.

"I didn't realize you'd want me to wait. I saw Wilkerson outside and wanted to see if he knew anything that would help O'Leary and my team with the case."

"Did he? Know anything?"

"He wasn't exactly cooperative. Until we figure out how all of these incidents are connected with Palmer, everyone is a suspect."

She put her hands on her hips. "*Everyone's* a suspect? You think Arlene, Wilkerson, Billy—don't deny it, I saw the suspicion in your eyes when you met him—heck, even the plumber is probably in on it. Oh, and Ken Taylor, my stable hand and temporary security guy. I'm sure you grilled him with questions inside the stable. Am I right?"

He didn't bother to deny it. Of course he'd questioned Taylor. And he'd question more of her ranch hands when he saw them. Right now, according to his talk with Taylor, most of them had left for the day and the rest would be gone by sundown. Which meant he'd just have to interview all of them tomorrow.

She must have seen the truth in his eyes. Her shoulders slumped as if in defeat.

"Colby, I appreciate everything you've done for me. But you can't just go around thinking every single person I come into contact with is involved in Palmer's schemes." She waved her hand toward her property. "I employ a lot of people. I don't want them to quit because they feel like I don't trust them. Promise me that tomorrow you won't interrogate everyone when they show up for work. I have a business to run. And I can't do that if you scare everyone off."

"You're way too nice for your own safety, you know that?"

She blinked. "I'm too nice?"

He sighed, then put his hands around her waist and lifted her up to sit on the top rail.

She squeaked in surprise and grabbed his arms to steady herself. "What are you doing?"

"Trying to make sure you listen and that you're taking this seriously."

Her gaze lowered to his lips and she swallowed. "Um. Okay. I'm listening."

He almost groaned out loud. Touching her, putting his hands on the sexy curve of her waist, even through her jacket, had set him on fire all over again. Now he was having trouble remembering what he wanted to tell her.

"Colby? You were saying?"

The husky tenor of her voice told him she was remembering their last kiss, just like he was.

He cleared his throat, and tried to focus, on anything but her mouth. "I'm saying that until Palmer and his men are caught, you need to be on your guard. You can't assume everyone is nice and doesn't want to hurt you."

"So I'm supposed to treat everyone with suspicion and be mean?"

"I don't think you could be mean if you tried. I'll settle for being suspicious and cautious, at least until we gather all the facts and figure out the truth."

"The truth. Do you even have a theory?"

"Working on it. Everything that's happened seems to have had a financial impact on your business. Maybe that's the goal. One thing's for sure. If Palmer just wanted to kill you, he could have done that with a rifle half a mile away while you walked your property."

She shivered and looked around. "Should we even be outside?"

"No one has tried to harm you here so far. I don't expect they will. Like I said, if that was the endgame, there was nothing to stop them." He glanced up at the darkening sky. "It's getting late. We should head back."

"I've got a golf cart at the stables that'll save us a long walk to the house."

They climbed the fence and headed across the hill.

"Are you hungry?" she asked.

"I could eat. Do you have another vehicle around here that we can drive into town? I'll buy you dinner at the restaurant of your choice."

"No need. Billy brought fresh groceries for us after I called him from Mountain City. He even stopped at one of my favorite barbecue places in town, Bradford's, and put two man-size dinners in the refrigerator to make sure we were taken care of."

"What a great guy."

Her eyes narrowed in warning.

He grinned. "Do you have sweet tea?"

"No, but I can make some."

"Barbecue and sweet tea. I just might be in heaven."

His phone buzzed in his pocket. After a quick glance at the screen, he answered. "Dillon, what's up?" He listened with growing unease. When Dillon finally finished, Colby said, "Okay. Thanks. I'll let her know." He ended the call and shoved his phone into his pocket. "There've been a few developments in the case. The first is that the search party found the bodies in the mountain."

"Wait, I thought they already found the man you stabbed."

"They did. Now they found Palmer's other two thugs. Both were shot. In the back. My guess is Palmer was eliminating loose ends."

"Oh, no."

"That wasn't all that Dillon had to share. Your ranch hand who was arrested earlier is singing like a bird."

"Arlene? She admitted to something more than busting the pipe?"

"A whole lot more."

"Wait, how would Dillon know what she said? Sheriff O'Leary's deputy is the one who arrested her."

"Based on what she told them, your sheriff wanted to consult with the sheriff of Johnson County, so he called and ended up talking to Dillon. Arlene confessed to being behind everything that's been going wrong on your ranch."

Piper pressed a hand to her throat. "That can't be. She's only nineteen or twenty years old, tops. She's been saving up to go to college in the fall. She's a good kid. I can't see her doing all that."

"I bet you couldn't see her taking a baseball bat to that pipe either, but there's a photo showing exactly that."

"I know, I know. Still, it doesn't seem real. Did she say why she did those things? Was she mad at me for something?"

"She was being blackmailed."

"I don't like where this is going."

"A couple of months ago she was waiting tables at a restaurant in town to save for college, like you said. She does want to start school in the fall, that part's true. What she didn't tell you is that she picked a few pockets on the side to help her save up for tuition faster. One of the customers in the restaurant saw her do it and snapped a picture. He used it to coerce her into applying for a job at your ranch."

"Which she did."

They started walking toward the stables again.

"She agreed to do one thing for her blackmailer, thinking that would be the end of it. But he took pictures of her doing that first thing and used that to threaten to anonymously turn her in to the police. From then on, she was stuck doing his bidding. He gave her a list of things to do and said she had to do at least two per week."

Piper nervously tapped a hand against her thigh as she walked. "Sounds about right. Did she say who was blackmailing her?"

"He never told her his name."

"Of course not. That would be way too easy, wouldn't it?" She sighed heavily.

"That's not the end of it. The sheriff showed her copies of all the sketches that Dillon faxed him earlier this morning. She positively identified her blackmailer. Guess who it was?"

She crossed her arms. "That's a no-brainer. Palmer."

"Nope. It was Jedidiah."

Chapter Sixteen

Piper shut the dishwasher and leaned back against the counter. "Jedidiah. I still can't believe he's a part of this. He let us go. And brought Gladiator back. Why would he do that if he's working with Palmer?"

Colby leaned against the counter opposite her. "Ever heard of Occam's razor?"

"It's the same thing as KISS—Keep It Simple, Stupid—right?"

His mouth crooked into a sexy grin. "Pretty much. The more complicated a theory becomes, the more assumptions you have to make for it to all come together, the less likely you are to be right. It all comes down to human nature. Vast conspiracies are too hard to maintain and fall apart easily. So the simpler explanation is generally the right one."

"In this case, what does that mean?"

"It means that Palmer and Jedidiah were probably working together initially, and now they've turned against each other. Palmer wanted you and me dead up in that mountain. He assigned his thugs to kill us. Jedidiah may have planned to kill us when he found us, but once he learned that Palmer was involved, he let us go. That leads me to believe they had a falling-out."

She nodded. "Makes sense. But I preferred the idea of Jedidiah being a nice person deep inside and that he let us go because you saved Mindy."

"You only see good in people, don't you?"

"Not at all. I'm not as naive as you seem to think I am. I just look at life through a more optimistic lens than you."

"Fair enough."

"How do you think they met?"

"Jedidiah and Palmer?"

She nodded.

"Most likely prison. We know Jedidiah did time. It makes sense he'd meet someone like Palmer behind bars. They're both career criminal types. But all of Jedidiah's sentences in Tennessee have been in local jails, not prison. So Blake's expanding the search to surrounding states. Once we figure out where he did hard time, if he did, we'll see who he hung with and if any of them meet Palmer's description. Plus, they both would have had to have been released two or more months ago like we theorized earlier."

"I don't remember hearing all of this when we were at the Johnson County sheriff's office."

"I had several long phone conversations with Dillon and Blake while you were snoozing on the trip up here."

At the reminder of the drive up, and her experiment, she cleared her throat. "Makes sense." She checked the digital clock above the stove. "Well, it's not too late by usual standards, just past eight thirty. But nothing about the past few days has been usual in any way for either of us. I'm going to call it a night. You're welcome to stay up as late as you want of course, but I'll go ahead and show you the guest room." She frowned and looked around. "Oh, shoot. The overnight bag you got in Johnson County is still in the truck isn't it? And Billy took the truck."

He straightened away from the counter. "I grabbed it before Billy left and stowed it in the stables. But I forgot to pick it up when I came back from Wilkerson's house. I'll go get it when I'm ready for bed. Mind if I use the golf cart later? I'm not quite ready to call it a night. Too keyed up."

"Of course, no problem. You don't have to ask." She crossed to him and opened the drawer next to his left hip and gestured to the keys inside. "I imagine you can use your mad detective skills to figure out which one is the right key."

He leaned over, his face inches from hers. "Hmm. I'm guessing it's on the key chain that's in the shape of a golf cart?"

"Give the man a medal."

She grinned, then her gaze fell to his lips, so close, so wonderful, so…hot. Instead of stepping back, as she should have, she stepped forward. Instead of him moving away, he moved closer. And then they were in each other's arms, like two magnets drawn together, helpless to resist the attraction between them.

Neither of them held anything back, as if they were both acknowledging that this was the last time they'd ever have this opportunity. That if they were ever going to assuage the molten craving that flowed between them, tonight was the night.

Tomorrow Colby would leave the ranch and work with the local sheriff and his fellow Destiny PD detectives to resolve the case. After that he'd go back to his life hundreds of miles away. But right now, this moment, he was with her. And for better or worse, no matter how crazy it seemed, she wasn't going to waste a single second of it.

They were gasping for air when Colby finally broke their hot, wild kiss. His hands were deep in her hair, his forehead against hers, chest heaving. Piper wasn't in any better condition. What had been a comfortably heated house moments ago was now stiflingly hot. She wanted to get naked. She wanted Colby naked. Her fingers clutched at his shirt, testing the buttons.

"This is crazy," he whispered. "Back in the truck, we told each other that—"

"Forget the truck."

"Piper—"

"Kiss me."

He groaned and covered her mouth with his in a ravenous display of passion and hunger that had her moaning deep in her throat. He scooped her into his arms, chest to chest, one hand supporting her bottom, the other cradling the back of her head as he lovingly devoured her.

She couldn't get enough of his kisses. But she wanted more. So much more. Her fingers found his buttons again and didn't stop until every one of them was undone. She splayed her hands across his naked chest. He jerked against her, breaking the kiss and then fastening his mouth against her neck. His hot tongue tasted her. His lips sucked against the sensitive skin. She cried out his name and his whole body tensed against hers.

"Condom," he rasped by her ear. "Please tell me you have a condom somewhere."

She laughed at his eagerness and slid her hands down, down, down between them. When she found him, she almost wept with the beauty and joy of the feel of him in her hands.

He shifted, giving her better access. "Don't tease me," he whispered against her neck. "I'll die. I swear I will."

She gave him one long stroke, reveling in the way he jerked against her and sucked in a breath.

"Piper."

"Down the hall. My bedroom's the last door on the left."

He turned with her in his arms and ran down the hall.

She stroked him again, down his considerable length, squeezing hard. He let out a curse and stumbled, almost dropping her.

"Do that again," he growled, "and I'll take you right here in this hall."

"Promises, promises," she teased.

He laughed and grabbed her wandering hand, then stumbled into her room.

"Where?"

"Should be in the nightstand, over there." She waved toward the left side of the bed.

"Should be?" He sounded like he wanted to weep as he hefted her in one arm and yanked the drawer open with the other. "Score." He grabbed the box, then coughed at the dust that swirled off it.

Her face flamed with heat. "It's been a while, okay?"

He grinned. "You were waiting for me, right?"

She pulled back and stared deep into his eyes. "I think I've been waiting for you all my life."

He swallowed hard and squeezed his eyes shut as if in pain.

"Stop thinking, Colby. Stop feeling guilty about a future neither of us can have. We have tonight. Don't waste it."

His eyes opened and he gently framed her face. "Piper, I—"

She pressed her lips to his, ruthlessly using his desire for her as her weapon. He shuddered in surrender, and then he was kissing her back with wild abandonment.

They both undressed in a frenzy, clothes flying across the bed, floating to the floor. She yanked the covers down, heard the sound of foil ripping. She quickly adjusted the pillows and turned around. He was there in front of her in all his glory, like a hungry panther ready to devour her. And, oh, how she wanted to be devoured by this man. But instead of pressing her back onto the mattress, he grew serious again and framed her face in his hands.

"Piper, sweetheart, I don't want you to regret this. I want you, more than you could possibly imagine. And I care about you, very much. But we both have different dreams, come from different worlds. I don't see how it could work long-term between us. I'd want you with me. Having you hundreds of miles away would kill me. If you want to stop, right now, I'll—"

She pressed her fingers against his mouth. "Colby, I'm a grown woman, not a fragile flower. Believe it or not, I *can* make love to you and still survive the next morning when you go off to your job and forget about me."

He frowned and pulled her hand from his mouth. "I didn't say I'd forget you."

"Well, you're not exactly saying 'I love you' either. But neither am I." This time she reached up and framed his face in her hands. "Colby, I care about you, too, or I wouldn't be doing this. I want you. I know what the future does—or doesn't—hold, and I still want you."

The uncertainty in his eyes almost made her melt onto the floor. What a sweet, wonderful man he was to be so worried about her feelings.

Could she really make love to Colby Vale and go on with her life tomorrow as if nothing had happened? Honestly? Probably not. She had a feeling there'd be an empty spot in her heart for the rest of her life. But it would be far emptier if she didn't love him when she could. She would bitterly regret never getting to hold him. If that meant she was half in love with him already, so be it. She'd deal with that later. But right now, all she wanted was to be held by this amazing man in front of her.

"Colby? Don't you want me?" She splayed her hands across his chest, delighting in how his muscles jerked when she touched him. If this was war, she'd fight with everything she had. She'd be downright ruthless. "I want you," she whispered.

That's when her panther pounced.

She was flat on her back and he was on top of her,

doing things to her body she'd never even dared to dream about before. He played her like a musical instrument, drawing her up, creating beauty unlike anything she'd ever experienced. He was the master and she was his most willing student.

He saw to her pleasure long before he worried about his own. And before the last tremors of her release had swept through her, he finally fitted himself to her and surged forward.

"Colby!" Her toes curled against the sheets as he drove into her over and over, his mouth hot against hers, his tongue making love to her mouth while his body made love to hers.

Just when she thought she'd die of pleasure, he thrust one last time and shouted her name, his entire body going taut. She climaxed all over again, and together they both floated down, down, down from the dizzying heights where they'd soared.

As his body went slack against hers, and his breathing deepened, he fell to his side, taking her with him, curling his body with hers in a protective embrace. She had never felt so cherished, so loved. And a long time later, when the afterglow finally faded away, she held him tight in her arms.

And wondered how she would ever let him go.

COLBY SAT STRAIGHT up in bed. Something had awakened him. But what? Then he heard it. The buzzing sound of his cell phone vibrating in his pants pocket. Only, his pants were on the floor somewhere in Piper's pitch-dark bedroom. His own bedroom had so many

LCD lights from the TV, video game consoles and DVR that it was lit up like a Fourth of July celebration.

He gently extricated himself from her deliciously warm, silky limbs and slid out of bed. A few seconds later he finally found his pants and grabbed the phone.

"Colby?" her sleepy voice called out behind him. "What's wrong?"

"Shh, go back to sleep." He glanced at the text message on the screen.

"Colby?"

"It's just Dillon, sweetheart. He was a little too enthusiastic about sharing progress notes on the case and didn't realize how late it is. Go back to sleep."

He grabbed his pants and hurried out of her bedroom, tugging them on as he made his way down the hall to the main room where her TV and electronics cast enough light that he could finally see. He plopped down on the couch and had just dialed Dillon's number when the overhead light flipped on. He blinked as his eyes adjusted.

Piper stood by the light switch in a Hello Kitty nightshirt, her arms crossed. He couldn't help but grin.

"Colby," Dillon said through the phone. "It's about time you returned my call. We—"

"Hold on." Colby tilted the phone away from his mouth. "I didn't mean to disturb you, Piper. I'll just go outside and talk to Dillon real quick." He stood and stepped toward the front door.

She moved to block his way. "No. You won't. My whole future is wrapped up in your investigation. I deserve to know what's going on."

"Colby?" Dillon's voice sounded from the phone, sounding impatient.

He hesitated, then sat back down on the couch. "You're right. I'll put him on speaker."

She blinked in surprise, then hurried over to sit beside him. "Thank you."

He set the phone between them. "Go ahead, Dillon. You're on speaker and Piper's here with me."

There was a pause, then, "Hello, Miss Caraway. Sorry to have disturbed you. Colby, you got my text?"

"I did. Why don't you repeat what it said, though."

"Okay. We were burning the midnight oil at the station and caught a few breaks in the case. We didn't get any good prints off the truck or trailer. All of them matched the kid that Jedidiah paid to drive the horses to the sheriff's office, which means Palmer or Jedidiah or both were smart enough to wipe everything down. So that slowed us down. But since we knew Jedidiah's real name, we were finally able to figure out where he recently did time. It was the Potosi Correctional Center, a maximum-security prison in Washington County, Missouri."

"Missouri?" Piper said. "That's a long way from Lexington."

"Six to seven hours, give or take," Dillon said. "Jedidiah got out of prison a few months ago, which corroborates what Arlene Garza said about seeing Jedidiah in Lexington around that time. Assuming he met Palmer in prison, we followed up on all known associates and got a hit. Todd Palmer, the fake one, is actually Shane Crowder. All we know so far about Shane is that he was in prison for robbing an armored truck."

"That's supposed to be impossible," Colby said.

"Yeah, well, long story but he and his buddies beat the odds. They got away with, you ready for this? Five million dollars."

Piper blinked in shock.

"How much time did he serve?" Colby asked.

"Not enough. The two armored-truck guards were murdered. Normally that would put the guys away for life, pretty much. But here's the kicker. The case was bungled from the start, all kinds of stupid mistakes. Which made it nearly impossible to prosecute these guys. And the money was never found."

"Never? As in, even now they don't know where it is?" Colby asked.

"Right. So our boy Shane makes a deal. He'll squeal on the other two so they can get nice, healthy long sentences, and he'll tell the feds where the money is hidden. In return, he serves no more than five years. The feds negotiate it to eight and make the deal. The trials move forward, Shane's two coconspirators are convicted of murder and they go to prison for life without parole. Shane gets his eight years in a separate facility from the guys he squealed on. Shane draws a map. The feds go into the wilderness and sure enough they find a buried safe right where he said they would." He hesitated. "You two still there?"

Colby said, "We're here."

"Okay. So another condition of the deal was that Shane's lawyer had the feds record the whole recovery so he could make sure they stuck to the agreement. If you watch the video, you can see them open the safe and you see a pile of money…and then, *bam*, a little explosion goes off and incinerates everything inside before the feds can even pull out one single bill."

Colby looked at Piper and could see his own amazement mirrored in her eyes. "So then what? Shouldn't Shane have gotten a life sentence at that point? And he should have been charged with setting up that decoy."

"Nope. None of that. True, Shane was a known explosives guy—from brief stints with construction companies and mining companies. But of course he claimed the other guys had set the trap and he didn't know that they'd done it. And his lawyer argued that Shane had stuck to the agreement, which his lawyer also pointed out was only to *tell* the feds where the money was. He never agreed that they had to actually recover the money. They were forced to keep their word. So even though the armored-truck company is out five million, or their insurance company is, and two men are dead, Shane gets his eight years. He was released right around the same time that Jedidiah was."

They were all quiet for a few moments, then Colby said, "I don't buy it. Shane wouldn't incinerate millions of dollars. He planted that safe as a decoy before he even robbed the armored truck, in case things went wrong. The money in that safe was probably fake, or he had real bills on top and everything under it was copier paper or something. He's got that five million dollars hidden somewhere. And if I think that, the feds have to think that, too. So why aren't they tailing him to see if he leads them to it?"

"What makes you think they aren't?"

"If they are, and they let him steal Gladiator and kidnap Piper and me, they're going to live to regret it."

Dillon laughed. "I'm with you on that. Of course they tailed our little explosives expert when he left prison. Which is why he needed Jedidiah to help him set up part of his next plan, at least until he shook his tail. Once he did, he disappeared."

Piper frowned. "While I think it's great that you've figured out all of this, I'm not seeing where I come into play. I haven't robbed any banks. I've never met either of these guys until the past few days. Why are they picking on me?"

"Your land," Colby and Dillon both said at the same time.

"My land?" Her face went pale. "Wait. You think Palmer, I mean Shane, buried the five million dollars on my ranch somewhere?"

"Yes," they both said.

"All the pieces fit," Colby told her. "Shane and Jedidiah were friends in prison. Friends talk. Shane knew the feds would follow him once he got out so he needed someone else to help him clear the way for him to dig up his money while he led them far away from where the money was hidden. As soon as the way was clear, he and Shane would dig up the goods, split the loot if they didn't kill each other first and disappear. But there's only one problem."

Piper crossed her arms over her chest. "Me. My ranch. And all the people I employ. He needs us gone so there won't be anyone to see him or stop him from retrieving the money."

"Exactly," Colby said. "All those accidents hurt your business so much that it doesn't even seem profitable on paper. My guess is that Shane wanted you to give up and shut the business down rather than try to sell it, which wouldn't have helped him. But he underestimated what a fighter you are. So he decided to steal Gladiator to lure you away so he could kill you up in the mountains. Probably because he didn't want this place to be a crime scene and have cops crawling all over it. Making you disappear worked better for his purposes. I imagine he would have given an anonymous tip after his thugs killed us, so the police would know you were dead. Then the ranch would be closed down and empty and he could do what he needed to do."

"But…" Piper's brow wrinkled with concentration. "Jedidiah didn't kill us in the mountains, and he returned the horses. So are they working together or not?"

"I think they had a falling-out," Colby said.

"I agree," Dillon said from the phone. "But that doesn't mean the enemy of my enemy is my friend in this case. I don't trust either of them."

"Me either." Colby automatically checked the pistol in his pants pocket, then wished he hadn't because Piper's gaze followed the motion.

She rubbed her hands up and down her arms. "What does all of this mean? You wouldn't have called at two in the morning unless you thought we were in danger, right? No one else is on the ranch this time of night besides Ken Taylor and me. And now Colby. You think Jedidiah or Palmer or both are coming here?"

Colby shook his head. "It's not likely, not with all the media alerts and the BOLOs that have been put out with Jedidiah's and Palmer's—I mean Shane's—

pictures plastered everywhere. They're probably both deep in the mountains waiting until they think the cops have quit looking for them. But we're not taking any chances either."

"Not taking chances how?"

"Blake and I are already on our way up," Dillon said. "As soon as the information started coming in, we headed your way. We'd been on the road for several hours before everything was confirmed. We're less than an hour out now."

She glanced at the curtain-covered windows, as if she could see through them. "What if they get here before then?"

Colby put his arm around her shoulders. "Neither of us think anyone's showing up tonight. But we're taking precautions. Dillon called Sheriff O'Leary and he's sending a deputy out tonight to stay with us. He should be here soon."

He could feel some of the stiffness drain out of her shoulders.

"That's good. Okay. Thanks." She gave him a shaky smile, then her eyes widened. "Wait, what about Ken? Someone needs to warn him to be extra careful."

"I'll call him. Is there anything else you wanted to tell us, Dillon?"

"That's pretty much it. We'll see you soon."

Colby ended the call and was about to ask Piper for Ken Taylor's number when a knock sounded on the front door.

Piper jumped, then pressed a hand to her throat.

Colby drew his pistol and pointed it toward the floor. "Stay down, be quiet," he whispered.

She nodded, and he stepped quietly to one of the front windows and flattened himself against the wall. Then he lifted the edge of the curtain and peeked out. He holstered his gun before looking back at Piper. "It's Deputy Hollenbeck from yesterday morning."

"Oh, thank goodness." Her eyes widened. "Oh, my gosh. I have to get some clothes on."

Colby grinned at the show she unwittingly gave him as she ran out of the room, her nightshirt bouncing up and revealing what she *wasn't* wearing underneath.

The knock sounded again. "Miss Caraway? Detective Vale? It's Deputy Hollenbeck."

Colby unlocked the door and pulled it open. "Hey. Thanks for coming out."

"No problem. I'm going to drive around the house and the outbuildings first, make sure everything looks okay. Then I'll veg out on the couch. Sound good?"

"Sounds great. There's a security guy at the stable. Name's Ken Taylor. I'll call him and let him know you're coming."

They shook hands and Colby locked the door again. He was about to call Ken when he remembered that he didn't have the man's number. He strode through the main room and down the hallway, stopping outside Piper's bedroom doorway to give her privacy.

"Piper, can you give me Ken's number?"

"Oh, sorry."

Her voice sounded muffled, like maybe she was pulling some clothes over her head. She gave him the number and he punched it into the phone and pressed Call. Nothing happened. He pressed Call again and checked the signal bars. Earlier there were five. Now there were none. He frowned and put the phone to his ear. Nothing.

Piper stepped out of the bedroom smoothing down a long shirt over some jeans. "Did you warn Ken?" She looked past him. "Is the deputy in the family room?"

"He's out checking the property." He looked at the phone again. Why would there be no signal whatsoever when he'd had no troble before? A cold hard knot settled into his stomach.

"Piper, do you have your phone handy?"

"Sure, is yours dead? I think mine still has juice." She disappeared into the bedroom and came back, carrying her phone.

"Call Ken."

She blinked. "You sound worried."

"I am. Call him. Now."

Her fingers flew across the keyboard and she held the phone to her ear, then frowned. "That's odd." She lowered the phone. "The call isn't going through. I've never had trouble making cell phone calls in my house."

Colby cursed and pulled her away from the doorway into the middle of the hall. "Someone's blocking the signals."

"Someone…" Her eyes went big and round. "Oh, my God."

"Do you have a safe room in the house?"

"A safe room? You mean with no windows or doors?"

"If that's the best you've got, then yes."

"My master bedroom closet, I guess."

He pulled her with him to her doorway, frowning because the closet didn't have a lock on the doorknob.

But it was still safer than her being in a room with a window. He reached in and shut the light off. "Okay, come on." He led her to the closet. "Sit on the floor. Do you have any guns?"

She shook her head. "No. I don't."

"No problem. You're going to be okay. Just stay in here with the light off. Wedge something under the door so it can't be pushed open from the outside. I'm just being extra cautious, not trying to scare you."

"Well, you're doing a lousy job if you're trying not to scare me." She ran a shaking hand through her long hair.

Colby kissed her hard. "Everything's going to be okay. It's probably just a bad cell tower."

"But you said—"

"Forget what I said. I'm just covering all our bases. I'm going to go out in the living room and wait for Deputy Hollenbeck to come back. Then I'm going to have him drive us into town, again, just to be certain that there's nothing to worry about. Okay?"

"O…okay."

He pointed to the light switch. "I'm going to turn this off before I open the door again. Once I close it, stuff clothes under the door. Got it?"

"Yes. I've got it. Go."

Bam! Bam! Bam!

Bam! Bam!

Colby cursed. "Piper, those were—"

"Gunshots. I know."

Bam! Bam! Bam!

"It sounds like the deputy is in a shoot-out. I need

to help him. Block this door and don't come out for anyone but me."

He yanked open the door and ran.

Chapter Seventeen

Colby crouched by the open car door and pressed his fingers against Deputy Hollenbeck's throat, searching for a pulse even though he didn't expect to find one. He shook his head and sent up a silent prayer as he closed the deputy's eyes. Did the man have a family? A wife, children waiting for him at home? To his shame, Colby hadn't even asked.

Hollenbeck's gun was still in its holster. He'd never fired a single shot. Someone must have sniped him through the windshield as he drove his car toward the tree line to the back right side of Piper's house. He'd never had a chance. But there had definitely been some kind of shoot-out. And it had been too close to the house to be coming from the stables. So who was shooting at whom?

A burst of static sounded from the police radio. Colby grabbed the mic to call for help. The cord dangled uselessly in the air, cut in two. He swore and tossed the mic into the passenger seat. That explained the open door. After shooting Hollenbeck, the shooter had leaned into the car and cut the radio cord.

A gurgling cough sounded from outside.

Ducking down, he eased around the open car door and saw what he'd missed earlier when he'd run to check on the deputy. Just inside the tree line, a man's body lay crumpled in the dirt.

Colby ran to him, unsurprised when he saw who it was. A gun lay discarded, several feet away. Colby kicked it into the woods, then dropped to his knees to see if he could do anything to stop the bleeding. But there was nothing he could do. Bullets had ripped through the man's chest and abdomen. Blood soaked his shirt, his pants, the ground beneath him. Air wheezed through a hole in his chest.

"Hell of a way to go, Jedidiah. What'd you do, come here with Shane to dig up your millions, and then you double-crossed each other?"

Jedidiah rolled his head back and forth. "Not *with* Shane." His voice was barely above a whisper. "Here to warn Piper. You. Tried to stop him." He coughed, then started choking on the blood.

Colby shoved his gun in his holster and pulled Jedidiah up on his lap, turning his head sideways to let the fluid run out of his mouth.

The coughing eased, and Jedidiah drew a deep breath. He smiled. "Knew you were a good man. You even help the bad guys. I'm sorry for what I did to you. To Piper."

"Yeah, well, everyone says they're sorry when they see the grim reaper knocking, don't they?" Colby scanned the woods, then back toward the house. "Who came with you? Just Shane, or does he have more thugs again?"

When Jedidiah didn't answer, Colby looked down.

The mountain man's eyes were open but unseeing. Air no longer wheezed out of his chest. He was gone.

Even though Colby doubted the man's sincerity, doubted that he was really there to help them, part of him hoped it was true and that Jedidiah had made peace with his maker before the end. He closed Jedidiah's eyes and said the same quick prayer that he'd said for the deputy. Then he eased the body onto the ground.

Another shot rang out in the distance. Then another. It sounded like they were coming from the stables. Colby jumped up, then hesitated. The stables were far away. If Ken was in trouble, he needed to get there fast. Colby had already arrived too late to save two men tonight. He didn't want to make it a third.

He ran to the open door and pulled the deputy out of the car. After gently laying Hollenbeck on the ground beside Jedidiah, he hesitated again. Then quickly unbuttoned the man's shirt. A minute later, he jumped into the patrol car and took off for the stables.

PIPER'S HANDS SHOOK so hard she was surprised that she didn't drop Deputy Hollenbeck's gun. Her father would have been ashamed that her training was so rusty. Then again, he'd probably understand since he'd accused her so many times of having too soft a heart. Tears streamed down her face as she turned away from the two dead men.

She didn't know what was going on or who had killed them. But she did know that the man who she'd finally realized she loved was out here somewhere with gunshots going off. And she wasn't going to cower in a closet while he faced *her* enemies without backup.

Bam!

She automatically ducked even as she realized that the latest gunshot was too far away to have been aimed at her. She drew a shaky breath and double-checked that her knife was in her back pocket. Then she climbed into the golf cart.

After carefully laying the huge gun on the seat beside her, she slammed the accelerator to the floor and took off at a teeth-grindingly slow pace toward the stables where the shots seemed to be coming from.

COLBY LEFT THE patrol car at the bottom of the hill, hoping for the element of surprise. He crept toward the stable's double doors, sweeping his pistol back and forth.

There'd been a spatter of gunshots less than a minute ago. But now they'd stopped. Did that mean that the fight was over? Had Ken Taylor managed to shoot Shane? Or the other way around? Or was there someone else out here, maybe more of Shane's jailhouse buddies?

A dark shadow ran from a tree to the right of the stable and pulled one of the double doors open. The lights inside illuminated his profile before he ducked behind the doors, but Colby would have known him anywhere.

It was Todd Palmer, aka Shane Crowder.

Which meant… Colby took off for the tree where he'd just seen Shane. When he saw the man lying there on the ground, obviously dead, he slammed the flat of his hand against the tree and cursed a blue streak.

He immediately regretted his outburst, realizing he may have just given up the element of surprise. And his hand was throbbing. But he was so sick of the waste of life. Ken Taylor didn't deserve to be murdered and left lying on the ground like yesterday's garbage.

Once again, Colby dropped to his knees and performed the now far too familiar ritual of closing a dead man's eyes and whispering a prayer over him. Then he climbed to his feet and reevaluated the situation.

He scanned the area again, then crouched down, keeping close to the stable until he could reach the next tree and retreat to the patrol car. There was no one else left to save except Piper. He'd leave capturing Shane to the local cops. He was going back to the house to keep Piper safe.

He'd just reached the double doors when they burst open and a horse ran out.

"Yaw!" someone yelled from inside.

Colby jumped back as more than a dozen horses ran out and galloped off into the night. The last one was a very familiar black stallion with a flowy main and tail—Gladiator. What the heck was going on?

He backed up some more, realizing he was a sitting duck if anyone came out the open stable doors. Just a few more feet and he'd be back at the tree.

Two dim lights shone ahead of him, coming up the hill from the direction of the house. Colby froze, immediately recognizing what it was. The golf cart that Piper used.

The buzzing sound of the electric motor reached his ears even before he could see well enough to make out Piper's form sitting in the driver's seat.

Shut it off, he'll hear you. Shut it off.

He crept forward and waved his arm, trying to get her attention. But she didn't seem to notice him. She'd stopped and was staring at the horses running across the fields downhill from the stables.

Colby moved forward again, glancing between the open stable doors and Piper. When he reached the opening, he leaned around the door to peek inside. Empty. Where had Shane gone? To the tack room? A stall? Maybe out the back door? Heck, he could even be upstairs in Ken's apartment.

He started to edge his way past the open doors to cut Piper off when he stepped on something hard and unyielding. An electric cord snaked beneath his feet. One end led to a stand of pines about forty feet from the front of the building. The other end ran straight through the stables, down the middle aisle, then off to the last stall on the left—Gladiator's stall. Why would someone run a cord through the stables?

The answer came to him in a flash. All of the puzzle pieces slammed together in his mind.

The stables were a little over eight years old.

Shane had served eight years for the bank robbery.

Which meant the foundation for those stables was poured right around the time that Shane stole five million dollars and it disappeared—somewhere on Piper's land. If someone buried something beneath several feet of concrete footing, how would they get it out? One way was dynamite. Shane Crowder was an explosives expert.

Colby whirled around and sprinted for the pines.

Was that laughter he heard?

Boom!

Searing heat slammed into him, tossing him into the air. The ground flew up to meet him at a dizzying speed. Then…nothing.

PIPER STARED IN shock at the hole in the stables where the back corner used to be, where Gladiator's stall used to be. Small bits of wood rained down like ash. And Colby, who'd been in front of the open double doors just seconds earlier, had been blown through the air and dropped to the ground, flipping end over end like a rag doll. And now he wasn't moving.

She shook herself into action and hopped out of the golf cart. After grabbing the gun, she took off in a sprint toward him.

Please let him be okay. Please let him be okay.

A sob escaped her as she dropped to the ground beside him. "Colby? Colby? Can you hear me, sweetheart?" She leaned over him. His eyes were closed and he lay on his side in the fetal position, facing away from her. "Colby?" She put her shaking hand to his throat, feeling for a pulse.

"He's dead, *sweetheart.*"

She jerked her head up, blood freezing in her veins when she saw who was standing over her. "Shane."

His brows arched in surprise. "You figured it out, huh? I'm impressed."

She swung the gun up toward him.

He cursed and grabbed her arm, giving it a brutal twist.

She cried out and the gun dropped to the ground.

He jerked her to her feet, his fingers like claws digging into the flesh of her upper arm.

"You got any more cops on the way?" His fingers squeezed harder.

Gritting her teeth against the urge to cry out, she shook her head. "N-no. I don't think so. Deputy… Deputy Hollenbeck was doing a routine check to make sure everything was okay." She tried not to remember how the officer had looked when she'd last seen him. If she thought about that, she'd be frozen with fear.

"Routine check, huh?" He laughed harshly. "More like he was looking for me, just like that stupid Jedidiah was." He said several foul things about Jedidiah and his questionable parentage. "We were supposed to split the money. But he developed a conscience, didn't want anyone hurt. How he ever made it in prison before I met him is beyond me. Got what was coming to him, though. He tried to ambush me." He leaned closer, his hot breath washing over her. "What an idiot."

She craned her neck, trying to twist back to look at Colby. Was he breathing? A sob caught in her throat.

Come on, Colby. Move. Do something so I know you're alive.

He shook her violently. "I told you he's dead. I saw him nosing around the stables and pushed the button at just the right time. Now it's just you, me and five million dollars."

He let her go and shoved her toward the stables. "Keep moving. You can help me load the money. It ain't as heavy as you'd expect, but there's a lot of it. It's in that stupid black horse's stall. Or what's left of it."

He laughed as he walked behind her. "Pretty clever,

burying it in the foundation if I say so myself. Kept it safe for me all these years. But figuring out how to get it out has caused me nothing but trouble. If you'd just closed the stupid ranch down, I could have gotten it without anyone hearing a dang thing."

Anyone except her neighbor Mr. Wilkerson. Then again, if Palmer—Shane—had been successful in his campaign to get her to give up on the ranch, he probably could have retrieved the money while Wilkerson was out of town. No one would have known until the property was being made ready for resale and they saw the condition of the stables with a hole blown in the side.

"Stop right there," Shane ordered.

They were just inside the entrance now. She turned around, desperately trying to see Colby through the open doors.

"I didn't say turn around." Shane pushed her shoulder and she stumbled backward, catching herself against the first stall.

"What do you want?" she demanded.

He laughed. "Now, there's that spunky *Piper Ann* from up in the mountains." His smile faded. "You're going to help me load those stacks of bills into the back of my truck. It's parked right outside the hole in that black horse's stall. If you try to run, trust me, you can't go faster than one of my bullets." He tapped the gun in the holster at his waist. "If you're nice, I just might keep you as a hostage until I'm good and out of here." He shoved her toward Gladiator's stall.

She climbed over debris and piles of sawdust, kicking boards and remnants of halters and bridles that had been blown off hooks on the walls out of her way. And the whole time she silently prayed for Colby and the one other person whose fate she was terrified to guess at—Ken Taylor. Was he upstairs, hiding? Or had Shane taken care of him the way he'd taken care of the deputy and Jedidiah? And Colby?

Her throat nearly closed with grief. Had she really thought that she couldn't use her knife on someone earlier? Because right now her fingers itched to pull her knife from her back pocket and show Shane just how good her aim could be. The image of Colby lying on the ground, eyes closed, would be all that she needed as motivation.

When she reached the back left corner of the stables, her mouth fell open at the extent of the damage. Not only was everything obliterated inside, but about ten feet of the exterior walls in both directions from the corner that used to be there were completely gone.

"Move," he ordered. "Get in that hole and start handing me money. And remember, you can't outrun a bullet."

The hole in the ground was a ragged L shape, following the line where the walls and their foundation had been. She climbed over yet another pile of wood and sawdust to reach it. An L-shaped metal box fitted neatly inside. What had once been its top was now a mangled, jagged piece of metal lying on the ground where it must have fallen after the explosion. And sitting inside the box were perfect stacks of one-hundred-dollar bills with bands around them.

"Pretty clever, huh?" Shane laughed. "Worked better than I ever dreamed. I had to rig a special compartment on top of the box for the dynamite. It had a V shape to angle the explosion up and out instead of down toward the money. I worked construction that summer and I'm the one who poured the cement back here."

Her entire body went cold. "There was dynamite under the walls all this time?"

"Yep."

"But…if I'd decided to expand the stables while you were still in prison, someone could have dug into the box and it would have exploded. They could have been killed."

He shook his head. "Nah. I kept tabs on this place. I would have found a way to stop you, even from prison." He waved toward the box. "It was the perfect setup. I just ran a line to the detonator and pulled it through a PVC pipe in the wall. Tonight all I had to do was connect another wire to that one and *boom*."

He laughed again, clearly impressed with his own prowess. "Obviously I couldn't let you expand the stables or someone would have found it. I had to scramble and move before I was ready because of your stupid plans." He shrugged. "But, hey. It all worked out in the end."

"Worked out? How many people have died for your schemes? How many people's lives have you ruined, like Arlene's?"

"Arlene?" He frowned in confusion. "Is she someone I killed? Can't say I remember that one."

She shivered at his cold disregard for human life. "The young kid you and Jedidiah blackmailed into causing all the problems at my ranch."

He snickered. "You can blame Jedidiah for that one.

I told him to wreck things around here to make you give up on the place and shut it down while I was trying to shake the feds off my tail. If he made someone else do his dirty work, that's on him."

He stepped over the hole in the floor and lowered the tailgate on a black 4x4 pickup parked outside. Had he knocked down a fence at the back of her property to get the truck inside? She certainly hadn't seen it or heard it approach the house.

It had a lockable top that could cover the whole back, but that was propped up on its hinges.

"Throw me some of those stacks of bills."

She looked around, then grabbed a piece of wood and set it across the box in the ground. Then she sat on it with her legs on either side of the hole and reached down for the money.

"Smart," Shane admitted. "I wouldn't have thought of that. Now, hurry up."

She tossed the stack to him and he tossed it into the back of the truck.

"Faster. More stacks."

It didn't take long before half of the money was in the truck.

He leaned over, his back to her as he shoved the bills farther into the truck bed to make room for more.

Piper braced her hands on the sides of the hole and hopped out. She scrambled over the debris and made it to the aisle.

Click.

"One more step and you lose your head."

She froze and then, very slowly, turned around.

Shane faced her from the other side of the hole, his

pistol leveled at her head. "We've got about two and a half million dollars left to load. You ain't done yet, Piper Ann. Get back here."

She hesitated. Once they finished loading the money, he'd kill her without a second thought. But Dillon and Blake were on their way, weren't they? How long ago had Dillon called? If she could stall him long enough for them to get here, maybe—

"In the hole," he bellowed, his face turning red.

"Why do you call me Piper Ann? That's not my name."

He frowned. "That's what your father called you."

"My middle name is Leigh. My dad's the only one who ever called me Ann. How did you know that?"

He shrugged. "Your mom and dad came over to visit me one day and I remember him talking about you. Your mom brought a batch of homemade cookies." He smiled as if reminiscing. "Man, they were good. She was nice, too. A real lady. Probably the only one I've ever met." His smile faded and he motioned with the gun. "But that don't mean I won't kill her daughter if I have to. Get over here. And shut up."

"But—"

Bam! The remains of a wooden post exploded beside her. She gasped and fell against what was left of the far wall.

"Next bullet goes in you," he promised, his eyes narrowing.

"Okay, okay."

Her heart slammed in her chest, the blood rushing in her ears. Her hands shook as she raked off chunks of wood clinging to her shirt and then stumbled over the debris back toward him.

Coughing at the sawdust in the air, she eased into the hole, facing the opposite direction to unload the money on the other leg of the L. She reached into the box and lifted a stack of bills.

"Drop the gun."

Piper jerked toward the familiar voice. Colby stood in profile in the opening on the outside the stables not far from the truck, aiming the deputy's gun at Shane's head.

He's alive, her mind screamed. But she didn't dare move or make any sounds. She didn't want to distract him.

Shane still had his gun in his hand from when he was pointing it at Piper. It was down at his side, aimed toward the ground. His body was still, like a deer poised for flight. But his eyes were busy, scanning everything around him. He was doing the same thing that Piper had done a few minutes earlier. Weighing his options.

"Toss the gun," Colby ordered.

Still Shane hesitated.

Piper held her breath, the tension so thick it seemed to be choking her.

Shane's gaze flicked past her, then he smiled and tossed the gun down. Not far enough away for Piper's peace of mind.

"You're tougher than you look, cop. Maybe I should have listened to my guy's excuses up in the mountain after all instead of killing him for screwing up. But then I had to kill both of them anyway to keep all my secrets safe."

The sound of his callous laughter over killing people made Piper's stomach clench with nausea.

"Are you okay?" Colby asked her without taking his gaze off Shane.

"Yes." She bit her lip to keep from asking the obvious next question: Was *he* okay? She didn't want to do anything that might turn his attention, or worse, make Shane think that Colby wasn't able to follow through with his threat to shoot him or control the situation.

"Get down on your knees, Shane. Lock your hands together behind your head."

Shane laughed. "You got some handcuffs from that stupid deputy? Is that what you're gonna do? Cuff me?"

"On your knees."

Shane's eyes narrowed and his smile turned feral. "And if I don't? You gonna shoot an unarmed man?"

"If I have to, yes."

Shane blinked. For the first time since she'd met him, Piper saw a look of fear pass over his face. But he quickly disguised it with his usual look of contempt.

"Okay, fine. I'm getting down on my knees, cop." He made a show of grunting and groaning as if he had arthritic legs as he lowered himself to the ground. "There, happy?"

"Hands behind your head."

Shane let out an exaggerated sigh and did as Colby told him. "You gonna cuff me now?"

"Piper," Colby said. "Come here. Stay to the far left, away from Shane."

She pulled herself out of the hole and scrambled up the pile of debris toward the left side of the ruined stall.

Chh-chh.

She froze at the deadly sound she'd heard in so many action movies over the years, the sound of a shotgun being pumped. Very slowly, she looked to her left. Standing in the aisle, out of sight from Colby, was a man pointing a long, terrifying-looking gun at her. A man whom she and Colby had both spoken to just hours earlier.

Mr. Wilkerson.

"I don't want to kill you, Miss Caraway. But I can't let your boyfriend kill that disgusting slimeball, even if he is my stupid bastard son."

His *son*? His illegitimate son?

Piper blinked in shock, glancing between son and father. There was no resemblance that she could see. But if Shane really was his son, then she finally had her answer for how he'd met her mom and dad. He must have been at the Wilkerson place at some time and her mom had insisted on taking over those now-infamous homemade cookies to welcome him. She blinked again. That was it—that boy who'd been next door during the summer for a few short weeks all those years ago. His name wasn't Dwayne as she'd thought while recounting the story to Colby. It was Shane.

He was the dark-haired nephew, only he wasn't a nephew. He was a son. And the Wilkersons hadn't wanted anyone to know. Because he wasn't Mrs. Wilkerson's son. What in the world had happened? Had they reluctantly taken him in for a few weeks, then shipped him off somewhere to keep his existence a secret?

"Detective," Mr. Wilkerson said. "Lower your weapon and let Shane go or I'm going to have to unload my shotgun into Miss Caraway."

She looked at Colby, a single tear spilling down her cheek. Fear wrapped its cold fingers around her heart and squeezed. But it wasn't fear for herself. It was for Colby. Because he was an honorable, wonderful man, a man she loved with all her heart. And she was terrified about what might happen to him.

"Don't do it, Colby. Don't lower your gun. Please. Just let me die. I beg you. Don't do it."

His jaw tightened and he looked at Shane, who was still on his knees, facing away from him, hands locked behind his head. Waiting, as they all were.

Piper let out a big sob and made a show of twisting and pulling at her shirt as if it was stuck on some debris. She wiped her eyes with her shirt, then tilted her right hand just enough to reveal to Colby the knife that she'd just slid out of her pocket.

His eyes widened, then he gave his head an almost-imperceptible shake. The meaning was clear. *No. Don't risk it.*

She nodded *yes* as she wiped her eyes.

Colby frowned and shook his head again.

She glanced at Shane and let out another sob, still pulling at her shirt. The tears were real. She was terrified that Colby was about to be killed.

"Shane?" Wilkerson called out, keeping his gun pointed at her.

Piper popped the knife open, staring into Colby's eyes.

Shane looked over his shoulder at Colby.

Colby looked at Piper and let his pistol fall to the ground. "Let her go, Wilkerson. I dropped my gun." And then, as if accepting that he had no choice but to trust her since she was obviously going to make a move anyway, he nodded.

"He dropped it," Shane confirmed, chuckling as he leaned over, reaching for his gun on the ground.

Wilkerson lowered the shotgun.

"Now!" Piper dropped her shirt and raised her knife. Colby and Shane both dived for their guns. Wilkerson's shotgun swung up as Piper threw her knife, as hard and straight as she could, just like her daddy had taught her all those years ago.

Bam! Bam! Bam!

Gunshots sounded from the opening in the ruined wall.

A guttural scream came from outside.

Old man Wilkerson dropped to his knees in the aisle, eyes wide with shock as he clawed at the knife handle buried in his throat.

Piper covered her mouth, both grateful and horrified that her aim was true.

Wilkerson's hands fell to his sides and he tumbled against the wall, then slid to the floor, dead.

Hands grabbed Piper's shoulders from behind.

"No!" She kicked out, twisting, trying to get away.

"Piper! It's me, Colby."

She looked over her shoulder at his beloved, beautiful face. "Colby." She sobbed, then climbed to her feet and turned, wrapping her arms around his waist. "Colby." She buried her face against his chest, barely registering what she'd seen behind him as she'd turned—Shane, lying on his back on the ground, his gun clutched in his hand, his sightless eyes staring up at the moon overhead.

"You're okay," she whispered. "Thank God you're okay."

"You took a terrible risk with your life." His voice sounded oddly strained and weak. "Don't ever do that again." He hugged her tight and kissed the top of her head. Then his arms went slack and he fell backward.

Piper blinked in shock. He lay like a marionette whose strings had been cut, his legs at an awkward angle beneath him.

"Colby!" She scrambled to him and ran her hands over his body, searching for injuries.

Shouts sounded from outside. Footsteps pounded on the ground.

"Colby? Where are you hurt?" She shook him. "Colby!"

Dillon and Blake were suddenly standing in the ruined opening of the outer walls of the stall, guns drawn, their chests heaving from exertion.

"Is there anyone else out here?" Dillon demanded, his frown creasing with worry as he stared at Colby.

"No. It's just us. I don't know what's wrong with him. There was an explosion. He was thrown, and there were so many gunshots. I don't know if… Help him. Please help him."

Dillon motioned to Blake. "Go. Get an ambulance. Get a chopper out here. Hurry."

Blake took off running.

Dillon leaped over the hole in the floor and dropped to his knees beside Colby.

Chapter Eighteen

Piper had to force herself not to interfere as the male nurse assisted Colby from the wheelchair into the rental car over a week after the debacle at her ranch. Her earlier attempts to be helpful had been a disaster. Colby was a big man and her measly five-foot frame wasn't quite capable of lifting him out of a wheelchair. All she'd succeeded in doing was nearly dumping him on the sidewalk.

At least she'd had the sense to rent a low-to-the-ground car for the trip to Destiny instead of bringing her truck. Colby never would have been able to climb up in that thing in his current condition.

"There," the nurse said, picking up Colby's feet and gently turning him to face forward in the passenger seat of the car. "Comfortable, Detective Vale?"

"I'm *fine*." He was still the grumpy patient he'd been since his first day in the hospital. He didn't tolerate needing help very well.

The nurse ignored Colby's bad attitude as usual. "Let me just get this seat belt—"

"I've got it." Piper nudged the nurse out of the way and pulled the shoulder belt over Colby. They'd already agreed the lap belt would be too uncomfortable pressing against his incision. He'd come so close to dying that night. If he hadn't put Deputy Hollenbeck's bullet-resistant vest on before he'd gone to the stables, the doctor said the blast would have shredded his organs instead of just rupturing his spleen.

She shook herself from her morbid thoughts and snapped the shoulder belt into place. Then she dropped a quick kiss on top of the adorable man's head.

He rewarded her with a frown. "I'm not a golden retriever."

She rolled her eyes and kissed him on the lips.

This time he rewarded her with a wink and a smile.

She backed out of the car and closed the door. After thanking the nurse and apologizing, again, for Colby's rotten attitude all week, she hurried to the driver's seat and got in.

"Ready?"

"Ready. Take me home, driver."

She pretended not to notice his dictatorial tone and accelerated away from the curb. "Have you considered getting in-home health care, a nurse who'll stop by every once in a while to check on you while you're recuperating?"

"I can take care of myself."

"So the doctor gave you permission to drive already in case you need anything?"

His silence was her answer.

"Like I said—think about getting a nurse to check on you now and then."

He grunted his reply and looked out the window. "Did Blake tell you what he found out about Wilkerson and Shane?"

"That Shane was the so-called nephew I told you about? Poor Mrs. Wilkerson. Her husband not only cheated on her, he ignored the product of that relationship—his son—until Shane was left orphaned and the state tracked him down as the father. I can't even imagine how that conversation went with his wife. And poor Shane, having to pretend he was a nephew and not even being openly acknowledged as the man's son." She shook her head. "No wonder he turned out bad."

"I'm not crying any tears over him. But I concede that being orphaned, ignored and shipped off to a boys' home without even being given his father's last name was a million ways of wrong."

She passed a slow-moving car and got back into the right lane. "I think it's sad no matter how you look at it. Shane was doomed from the start with a crackhead mom and a father who was already married and refused to acknowledge him."

She glanced in the rearview mirror. "Shane said he kept tabs from inside the prison, that he could have stopped me if I'd tried to expand the stables before he got out. Do you think it was his father who updated him on what was going on? If so, why would he do that when he ignored his son before he went to prison? Did he feel guilty after his wife died and decided to protect his son in any way that he could? Even by killing for him at the very end?"

Colby shrugged. "A guilty conscience might explain Wilkerson's actions. Or maybe he wanted some of that money for himself and figured the only way to get it was to help his son. I don't guess we'll ever know." He motioned toward an exit. "Let's take that county road for fun."

"For fun? I've never even been down that road. I don't know where it goes."

"Humor me."

She put her blinker on, shaking her head as she headed down the off-ramp. "Okay. Which way? Left or right?"

"Left. That looks like it should take us somewhat parallel to the highway but we'll get to see some pretty scenery."

"Pretty scenery. Are you sure the pain medicine isn't making you loopy? This detour could take us miles out of our way."

"Is there something at the ranch you have to get back to by a certain time?"

The ranch. Her hands tightened on the steering wheel.

"Piper?"

"What? Oh, sorry. No, no. There's nothing at the ranch that I have to worry about." She forced a smile.

An hour passed with only the sound of the rushing wind to break the silence inside the car.

A sign up ahead announced an intersection. Piper slowed. "What do you think? If we've been going parallel to the highway, we should be about halfway to Destiny now. But I'm not sure whether we should continue straight or go left again."

"Go straight, then turn right at that sign up there."

"Sign? I don't see a sign."

"You will." He sounded ridiculously pleased with himself.

She looked over at him, then pulled straight ahead. "Did someone double your dosage?"

He laughed. "Just pull in there." He waved to the right.

Sure enough, there was a sign where he'd said there would be—letters on an archway that spelled Second Chance Ranch. She pulled the car to a stop.

"I don't think we should go in there. It looks like someone's private property."

"Do you trust me?"

"What?"

He pulled her right hand off the steering wheel and pressed a kiss on top of it. "Do you trust me?"

She swallowed and stared at her skin, still feeling the burn of his lips. "Um, yes?"

He laughed and let her hand go. "I know the owner. It's okay. Just pull up to the house. I want to show you something."

She would have argued, but he looked so happy and peaceful and so dang sexy that her mouth watered for wanting him. Oh, how she loved this man. But did he love her? That was the question. They'd agreed there was no future for them. But that was before the explosion, before she'd spent nearly every waking hour at his side, praying for his recovery. And yet, here she was, driving him home so he could leave her. Didn't that answer the question about whether he loved her or not?

"Piper, the house? It's just past that curve."

She nodded and pressed the gas, easing down the long road into the property. There were pristine white three-rail fences running on either side, just like the fences at her ranch. But where her land was winter-brown, this land was a vibrant green. It had been seeded with winter ryegrass.

Giant oak trees spread their thick branches toward the sky. Devoid of leaves now, they'd be lush, heavy shade trees come the spring. She could easily imagine a dozen horses running behind these fences, standing under the trees, sipping from the sparkling pond in the distance.

"It really is beautiful here."

"Yes. Beautiful."

He was smiling when she looked at him.

She frowned and stopped the car. "Colby? What's going on?"

His long-suffering sigh could have knocked her over if she'd been standing.

"Okay, okay." She pressed the gas and hurried around the curve. A small white clapboard farmhouse with a wraparound porch greeted them. Its black shutters provided a stark yet homey contrast to the blindingly white house. A porch swing gently moved back and forth in the light breeze at the far left end of the porch.

"Is your friend home?" she asked. "Is he…or she…expecting us?"

Without answering, he unclipped his seat belt and pushed his door open.

"Colby, wait." She hurried out of the car and ran to his side, just in time to help him stand. "Are you sure you should be walking? I can try to get closer to the porch if you want."

"This is perfect right here." He turned around, pulling her with him to face the acres of beautiful pastureland spread out before them.

"Who lives here? Did your brother, Scott, buy this place and move out here? Did Joey finally make it big in Nashville, and he and Lisa are here?" She tried to look over her shoulder at the house but his arm tightened, keeping her from turning around.

"You are a very difficult person to surprise, Piper Ann Leigh Caraway. Just be quiet for one more minute." He glanced at his watch. "Yep, we're right on time. Just wait."

His vague responses were driving her crazy. She was just about to demand that he explain everything when the sound of hooves pounding against the ground glued her to the spot. The gait was distinctive, heavy, like a draft horse might make. And then the horse burst into view, crossing the pasture from right to left, its thick black mane and tail rippling out behind it.

Her mouth dropped open in astonishment, then her vision blurred as tears slid down her cheeks. "Gladiator? Why is he here? I sold him two days ago. I don't understand."

Colby gently turned her to face him and tilted her chin up. "Yes, you did. You sold your ranch, too."

"But...how did you know?"

"I'm a detective."

"A detective who's been in the hospital for the past week. Who told you?"

"Your ranch manager may have paid me a visit."

"Billy? Why? What did he say?"

"That I was an idiot to let you go and return to Destiny alone. And that you were an even bigger idiot for selling off everything to follow me like a nomad in the hopes that I might come to my senses and realize that I was in love with you."

She blinked. "He called me a nomad?"

He laughed and feathered his thumb across her

lower lip, making her shiver. "Was that what you were going to do? Move to Destiny to try to convince me that we were meant to be together?"

Her face flamed with heat and she looked away.

"Piper."

"When you say it out loud, I sound really pathetic."

"Never. Especially when you realize that I sold my farm in Destiny two days before you sold your ranch in Kentucky."

Her mouth dropped open again. "Wait. What? You sold your home? But...but I was driving you home."

"Yes, you were. And you have."

He turned her with him to face the farmhouse. "Welcome to my new home, exactly halfway between *my* old home and *your* old home. *Our* home, if you want it to be. I never wanted you to give up your dream, to give up your ranch. It's probably not too late if you want to cancel the sale and try to—"

She pressed a finger to his lips, stopping him. Her heart was full, near to bursting from the moment he'd called this place "our" home.

"Colby, you told me once that you wished your sister hadn't given up her dream to marry Joey. But she didn't give up her dream. She found a new one. A better one. I don't need the ranch to be happy, Colby. I just need a better dream." She stared up at him, waiting, hoping.

He drew a shaky breath, his arms tightening around her. "I love you, Piper. If you'll have me, I'd like us to build that better dream together, to build a life, create our own family here, together. That is, if you don't mind a small-town cop having to move up the ranks in a brand-new county and a brand-new town." He reached into his pocket and pulled out a shiny silver shield. "I'm a brand-new deputy out here, starting over. And I'd love for you to start over with me as a new rancher. So what do you say? Will you marry me?"

The tears were flowing hard now. "You love me?"

"Oh, sweetheart. I love you more than anything and I always will. Yes, I love you."

She smiled so hard her face hurt. "I love you, too. With all my heart. So my answer is—"

"Wait, hold that thought." He shoved the shield back in his pocket. "I knew I'd mess this up." He patted his other pants pockets, then dug his hand inside the left one.

"Colby?"

"Just a second."

He pulled his hand out and held up the most beautiful ring she'd ever seen. Little diamonds sparkled all over the top in the shape of a horseshoe.

She drew in a sharp breath. "It's beautiful. But how did you—"

"That day my sister drove up to the hospital from Nashville, then left ridiculously early and you were mad at her for not visiting me longer? Remember that?"

Her face flushed with heat again. "Oh. No. Don't tell me she ran around helping you set all this up, and I was angry with her."

"No worries. She understood why you were snippy."

She gasped. "I wasn't!"

He grinned. "You totally were. But she'll get over it. I told her what I wanted and she was more than happy to spend my money on jewelry." He waved his hand toward the grounds. "I bought this over the internet. The actual closing doesn't happen for a few more weeks but the owner is letting me rent it until it's official. So it's basically mine. Ours. If you want it to be."

"Oh, Colby. I had no idea. I wasn't even sure whether you loved me."

"Remind me to tell you I love you every day for the rest of our lives, if you'll agree to be my wife."

He started to lower himself to one knee and she grabbed his arm.

"Don't you dare. I'll never be able to help you back up."

She pushed his hand toward her left one and he slid the ring onto her finger. She held it up, admiring the way the horseshoe glittered in the sunlight.

"Is that a yes?" he teased.

She blinked. "Oh! Yes, yes! Definitely a yes." She threw her arms around his neck and kissed him. He thoroughly kissed her back and hugged her so tightly she was gasping when they broke apart.

"We're home then?" She smiled up at him. "We get to stay here?"

"We're home. I may even have a plan for getting up those steps to the front door." He winked, then straightened and turned her once again toward the pasture, where Gladiator was calmly grazing out by the pond. "Just one more thing. I thought it might be a little difficult to start a new ranch without livestock, so…" He raised his hand and waved.

Seconds later, the sound of hooves pounded on the ground again. *Many* hooves. Gladiator raised his head, staring off toward the right side of the property, just past the house. And then a half-dozen horses raced into view, white stockings flashing, manes blowing in the wind.

Piper sucked in a breath. "You didn't!"

"I did. I had Billy buy back six of your favorites. I couldn't afford more than that. Oh, and just to be completely honest, I couldn't afford Gladiator either. I more or less leased him for a bit. I'm hoping some of the money you got from his sale can be used to officially buy him back."

She laughed and threw her arms around him again. "I think that can be arranged. Now, why don't you tell whoever's been helping you with the horses to get over here and help me get you up those steps?"

He grinned and waved in the air again. A man jogged out from behind some bushes at the corner of the house grinning at her in the same adorably lopsided way that Colby often did. Piper had met him at the hospital, too. He was Colby's brother, Scott. She grinned back. After all, how could she not? He was family, soon to be her family.

Tears of joy flowed down her face as she stared up into the eyes of the man she loved. "Take me home, Colby."

And he did exactly that.

* * * * *

"What are you saying? That instead of accepting that they could
be lost in the woods, you think someone came up here and...what?
What did he do with them?"

"No, I'm not saying that at all. I'm just throwing out the facts
as we know them. The team drove up but didn't drive back down.
They aren't answering their phones, radios or us yelling at the top
of our lungs. Something bad must have happened."

Her voice was barely above a whisper the next time she spoke.
"I think we may be in over our heads. We should call the station,
get some volunteers out here to help us conduct a more thorough
search. Even if they're not lost, they could be stranded somewhere,
maybe in a cell phone and radio dead zone. Obviously something
happened to them or their vehicles wouldn't still be here."

"Agreed. We need to get some help out here."

He raised his flashlight beam, training it straight ahead, slicing a
path of light through the darkness of trees and bushes about twenty
feet away. "While you make that call, I'm going to go deeper in
to check that barn and the clearing in front of it. There have to
be some footprints there, maybe a piece of torn fabric caught on
a branch. I'd like to find some tangible proof that might show us
where the team was last. The trackers will want to start from the
last known position."

She shoved her cell phone back into her pocket. "We're not splitting up. I'm your partner. We'll check it out together. Then I'll call this in."

The wobble in her voice had him hesitating. He looked down at her, noted the intensity in her expression, the shine of unshed tears sparkling in her eyes. He'd been with Destiny PD since late fall of the previous year and had been her partner for over four months. In all that time, she'd always been decisive, in control, never breaking down no matter how tough things got. He'd never once seen her rattled. But right now she seemed…fragile, vulnerable. And he'd bet it wasn't just because she was worried about her friends. There was something else going on here. And he thought he knew what it was.

"Donna?"

"Yeah?"

"It's not your fault."

She frowned. "What's not my fault?"

"Whatever happened, whatever is going on with the team. I think you're second-guessing yourself, feeling guilty. But if anyone's to blame, it's me. If I'd been a good partner to you, we'd have both been here with them when—"

"When what? When aliens beamed them up to the mother ship? Come on, Blake. This is crazy. Four highly trained SWAT team members and the chief of police don't just disappear off the face of the earth. You know what I'm starting to think is going on? Group hysteria, or mass hysteria, or whatever psychologists call it. We're both feeding off each other's fears and making this into something it's not."

"I honestly hope you're right."

See what happens next when SWAT STANDOFF by award-winning author Lena Diaz goes on sale in June 2018 wherever Harlequin Intrigue books are sold!

www.Harlequin.com

LOVE
Harlequin
romance?

Join our Harlequin community to share your thoughts and connect with other romance readers!

Be the first to find out about promotions, news, and exclusive content!

Sign up for the Harlequin e-newsletter and download a free book from any series at

www.TryHarlequin.com

CONNECT WITH US AT:

Harlequin.com/Community

 Facebook.com/HarlequinBooks

 Twitter.com/HarlequinBooks

 Instagram.com/HarlequinBooks

 Pinterest.com/HarlequinBooks

ReaderService.com

**ROMANCE WHEN
YOU NEED IT**

HSOCIAL2017

Earn points from all your Harlequin book purchases from wherever you shop.

Turn your points into *FREE BOOKS* of your choice
OR
EXCLUSIVE GIFTS from your favorite authors or series.

Join for FREE today at
www.HarlequinMyRewards.com.

Harlequin My Rewards is a free program (no fees) without any commitments or obligations.

MYR17

THE WORLD IS BETTER WITH

Romance

Harlequin has everything from contemporary, passionate and heartwarming to suspenseful and inspirational stories.

Whatever your mood, we have a romance just for you!

Connect with us to find your next great read, special offers and more.

f /HarlequinBooks

🐦 @HarlequinBooks

www.HarlequinBlog.com

www.Harlequin.com/Newsletters

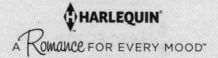

⬨ HARLEQUIN®

A *Romance* FOR EVERY MOOD™

www.Harlequin.com